I0543261

Not a Word

By Dawn Sister

Beaten Track
www.beatentrackpublishing.com

Not a Word

Second Edition
Published 2018 by Beaten Track Publishing
eBook first published 2015 by MMRomanceGroup
Copyright © 2015, 2018 Dawn Sister

All rights reserved.

No part of this publication may be reproduced, stored in a retrieval system, or transmitted, in any form or by any means, without the prior permission of the publisher, nor be otherwise circulated without the publisher's prior consent in any form of binding or cover other than that in which it is published and without a similar condition including this condition being imposed on the subsequent publisher.

The moral rights of the author have been asserted.

ISBN: 978 1 78645 265 8

Beaten Track Publishing,
Burscough. Lancashire.
www.beatentrackpublishing.com

Contents

Not a Word

Chapter 1

In which I meet my new neighbour

WHAT THE HECK? I take the dog out in the car for one of our longer walks, and when I come back two hours later, the entire street is blocked with removal trucks.

Who's moving? And are they moving in or out?

I never take any notice of what goes on in the street. I haven't really been interested for a long time. I keep to myself and no one bothers me, which suits me just fine.

Today, though, I can't get into my drive because there's a great big furniture removal van blocking it.

What am I supposed to do now? Getting the truck moved would mean speaking to someone, and I can't do that on the best of occasions. When I'm stressed, it's even harder.

Two men, with perhaps more tattoos than actual bare skin, walk past me, carrying a large red, garishly patterned sofa. I try to get their attention.

"Er-er, ex-excuse m-m-m-m-me!"

"Watch it, mate. There's work goin' on here."

Before I can get another word out, they've disappeared into the house next door to mine. My dog gives a low, menacing growl, far too late for either man to be concerned.

"That's right, growl at them, Zen. Potential murderers, are they? You're such a hard case, waiting for them to get out of earshot before you threaten them with impending death." I chuckle as my three-year-old Jack Russell looks up at me with pricked-up ears and a stupid, tongue-lolling grin.

At least the fact that they carried the sofa into the house explains what's going on. They wouldn't exactly be moving furniture into the house if someone was moving out.

Now, I know I'm not a terribly good neighbour, but I would at least have the courtesy to let my fellow neighbours know if I was moving out. The fact that a neighbour's departure went unnoticed by me makes me feel a little guilty, although I'm not the most communicative of people, which in turn, I suppose, makes people not want to communicate with me.

That arrangement actually suits me fine, unless it is a situation like this, where I need someone to do something for me, like move a damn truck that is blocking my drive.

The two tattooed men come back out of the house, followed by others. None of them look particularly happy to see me standing in their way, but until I can get into my drive my car is parked in the middle of the road. What am I supposed to do?

"I-I-I…" I begin, but I'm interrupted by tattoo guy number one.

"Look, sunshine, we don't 'ave time for this. We've got two trucks to empty in less than an hour, so could you get out of our way?"

"B-b-b-b-but, I l-l-l-live h-h…" Urgh! I give up.

A car horn toots, and I realise I am causing an obstruction now. I groan and shrug as the men sneer at me like I'm some sort of *retard*. I get that a lot, so it kind of goes over my head. I sidestep to get around them and move to my car. They forget about me and my little dog and get back to work.

Less than an hour and then I'll be able to park in my drive. I guess I can cope with that.

I pack Zen back into the car and drive up the street to find a parking space until the trucks have moved.

Walking back down the hill with Zen, I get a good view of the removal men without them noticing I am watching them. They're all rather too muscular and beefy for my taste. Too many tattoos.

"Those guys have so many damn tattoos. I doubt there's a piece o' skin that hasn't been inked."

I whirl around and come face to face with a tall, slim, young man leaning against a tree that borders my front garden. He is lurking in the shadows, which is why I didn't see him at first. He's also watching the men at work whilst flicking through screens on his phone. He pockets the device and steps out into the light. The sunshine lights up his sandy-coloured hair which is feathered around his face to frame deep-blue eyes and a pleasant, upturned mouth.

Was he actually talking to me? Or was he just making a comment as I passed? And what was his accent? American? I detected a distinct drawl. Before I can even begin to formulate a reply, he speaks again.

"Is this your dog?" The man, kid really, since he can't be more than twenty at the most, crouches down to make a fuss of Zen. "I used to have a Jack Russell when I was a kid. He was called Mixer. Don't even ask me why. Dad named him. What's yours called?" He's looking at the collar as Zen tries very hard to lick his hand and halfway up his arm as well. "Hmm, Zen." He nods as he reads the disc without waiting for me to reply. "Hello, Zen. You're an excitable little thing, aren't you?" He chuckles.

Well, I suppose he's saved me the embarrassment of having to stammer out Zen's name, although 'Z's are one of the letters I find easier to say.

"Hi, I'm Zak!" He jumps up and holds out his hand for me to shake. "It's Zachary really, but everyone just calls me Zak. I just moved into the street. Well, into the country, actually, about three weeks ago…" He rolls his sparkling eyes, and the action makes my breath hitch. "What I mean is, my mom and I just moved into the street. We're from San Diego. My mom was born over here, and she wanted to be close to family because—well—just because. I said I'd come with her. I could've stayed to finish college, but I would've been on my own for over a year, and that sucked balls. I have dual nationality, so I can study just as well over here, which is pretty cool, huh? My aunt, that's my mom's sister, she lives about ten miles away. They're starting a catering business together. I have a ton of cousins I need to get to know. Do you live around here, or are you just walking your dog in the neighbourhood?"

Oh my god, I think he just told me his life story without taking a breath. That was quite an incredible feat, and I'm rather impressed, except now he'll want me to tell him mine, or my name at the very least. What a chore! I'm trying not to get into a panic about it, but when your name is Niall and you can't actually say it without getting stuck on the 'N' for about five minutes, it becomes a bit of a joke.

I swallow hard as he regards me with anticipation. I try not to notice how thick and long his eyelashes are, or how his smile shines brighter than the sun. My mouth has suddenly gone very dry. I take a breath, open my mouth and then grimace in apology before I sweep Zen into my arms, retreat up the steps of my porch and into my house before Zak can even register what's happened.

Standing with my back against the door and breathing rather heavily, I think it may have been excessively dramatic to run off like that. I'm forty-three, for goodness' sake. I shouldn't be doing things like this, but he was staring at me with those sapphire eyes, and my brain just went 'pop'. Did I imagine him? Because he's bloody gorgeous. Slim, blonde, beautiful. And that accent! *Hngh!* But he's so young! What the hell is going on in my head?

I should've at least tried to talk to him. He's my new next-door neighbour—not that being on good terms with my neighbours has ever been a priority before, but there's always a first time. Maybe I should go back out there and apologise. I hardly made the best first impression. What must he think of me? Not only is he new to the street, he's new to the country. He must think British people have rods up their arses.

Of course, there's always the possibility he'll stop being so friendly once I open my mouth. People tend to back off with embarrassed excuses about having to be somewhere else when they hear my attempts to hold a decent conversation.

The way I scowl and grunt tends to scare people off. I have a reputation for being uncommunicative, but in reality I just prefer for people not to know I have the world's worst stutter. It's easier for them to think I'm grumpy and sullen than for them to think I'm broken.

I nearly jump out of my skin when the doorbell rings. I place a hand on Zen's head to stop him from barking and giving away that I am right behind the door.

"Er, hello?" a voice calls from the other side of the door. The call is followed up by a knock. When I don't immediately reply, the letterbox flap opens and Zak calls through. "Sorry if I freaked you out, man. I didn't mean to. God, I didn't know you would run off or anything like that. I didn't think I was that scary, and you didn't look like a flight risk. Mom says sometimes I'm a bit forward and I talk too much, but I didn't, did I? Not just then, anyway. And you're a neighbour, so I should be trying to make a good impression. Mom'll kill me if I've screwed up in the first ten minutes of getting here. I didn't catch your name, I bet it's awesome. I'll get it next time, I'm sure."

"Zachary Cartwright! Where in hell are you?" a woman's voice calls from a distance, and the kid curses. "Come and help with the move or so help me I'll stick your stuff out in the yard."

"Shit. Zachary Cartwright. That's me. I only get my full name when I'm in trouble. What am I, a little kid? Jeez!" For some reason I have an image of him rolling his eyes as he peers through the letter flap. "I gotta go. Please don't hate me, Mr. Neighbour. I think your dog is cute as fuck. Shit, I didn't mean to swear. Mom says I cuss too much, crap... I should just stop because I don't think my foot will fit any further into my mouth. See you round, er, whatever your name is. Oh, and Zen—see ya, Zen."

I heave a sigh of relief as I hear footsteps bounding away from my porch. I had actually been about to answer the door, if only to stop him talking. I don't think he took a breath. It was kind of funny, really. I feel myself beginning to laugh. It was more than funny; it was hilarious.

"And what about you, Zen, eh?" He licks at my hand as I make a fuss of him, the grin broadening on my face. "Here I am, trying for aloof and enigmatic, and you're treating his arm to a tongue bath, you slutty mutt."

Zen just hangs out his tongue like he's laughing at me. The joke's on him really, because once our neighbour has discovered I'm not the talkative type he'll leave us alone. They all do in the end.

Chapter 2

*In which my new neighbour
finds a hole in his fence*

THE NEXT DAY, I'm trying to work in my garden, but it's hot—definitely too hot to do anything involving moving about. It's unseasonably warm for May, and after about two hours of sweaty labour in my flower beds I take a break.

It's so warm I have to sit in the shade. I relax and enjoy the peace with a book and a well-earned, cold beer.

I can hear a lawnmower buzzing away, and I think it's coming from next door. The previous neighbours weren't that great at mowing their lawn, so the new ones have their work cut out. I can't help wondering if it's Zak. I wonder if he's as scorched as I am working in this heat.

I try not to wonder what he looks like all hot and sweaty, because—*where the hell did that thought come from? You dirty old man!* I must be twice his age at least. Doesn't stop me looking though, or thinking. Or imagining. Oh my.

Zen is somewhere in the garden. He's up to something. I can hear him snuffling and growling. The noise is irritating.

"Zen, what are you doing?" I look up from my book just in time to see his front end disappear under the fence that separates mine and next door's garden. "Oh, shit!" I jump up and try to reach him before he completes his escape, but no such luck.

7

I kneel down at the base of the fence and inspect his handiwork.

"God, Zen, what a bloody mess." I stick my hand through the hole, but he's out of reach. I now have visions of him rampaging about in the new neighbour's flower beds and causing all sorts of havoc.

Thankfully, the lawnmower noise has stopped. I'm hoping that means my neighbour has gone in. Maybe if I call Zen he'll come back through the gap, and I can block it up before anyone notices.

I lie down and peer sideways through the gap. I can only fit my face through. How on earth did Zen fit through there? I suppose he is a Jack Russell, so he was bred for squeezing through tight spaces.

"Zen!" I hiss, trying to see where my wayward mutt has got to. I can't see him, but I can hear him, snuffling and growling and barking excitedly at something. "Zen, come here, you silly dog. You'll give a bad impression, for goodness' sake."

"Hello again!"

Oh god, I've been rumbled!

A pair of feet, wearing scruffy canvass trainers and belonging to some very nice, very masculine legs, stand to the left of the hole Zen has created beneath our dividing fence. Slowly, my eyes wander up to look into the face of the young man I met and ran away from yesterday.

"Remember me?" Zak is leaning against our dividing fence, drinking from a water bottle. He wipes his mouth and grins. "I never did catch your name. It's a lovely day, isn't it?" He's smiling down at me as if it's the most natural thing in the world to see your neighbour's face forced through the base of your fence. "Are you missing a dog, by any chance?"

I open my mouth to speak, then panic and pull my face away from the hole with a gasp.

"Do you want me to push him back through?" Zak offers. "Or would you prefer him to come home via a more conventional route?"

I'm sitting beside the gap with my back to the fence, biting my lip and blushing furiously. Suddenly his face appears through the hole I've just vacated.

I stare down at his bright, youthful expression. His eyes are twinkling and he's grinning from ear to ear. I can't understand what he's finding so funny, unless it's my utter discomfort and embarrassment.

"Hi!" He flicks his eyebrows as I continue to stare. His gaze wanders, taking in my garden, or what he can see of it from that angle. "Wow, you have an amazing garden!" He gasps. "Ours is a fucking jungle. Want me to bring Zen round?"

Before I can answer him, he's disappeared to, I assume, 'bring Zen round'.

Oh god. Now what? I'm going to have to speak to him, and then he'll think I'm a real headcase because I can't string more than two words together—unless I'm talking to Zen.

There's a knock at my door before I'm even inside the house. I find myself running to answer even though I know for certain this is going to be the most excruciatingly embarrassing and awkward meeting ever.

"Greetings, neighbour." Zak grins as he steps into my entrance hall, holding a squirming Zen in his arms. "Okay, little feller, don't be such an eager beaver." He places Zen on the floor, and my errant dog jumps about his feet like he's greeting an old pal. "What is it, little guy?" Zak laughs and crouches down to make a fuss of him. "You are so cute. Digging a hole in your master's garden… I bet he's really pissed at you."

Zen is just being a complete and utter dog whore and is now rolling on his back, getting his stomach rubbed.

Zak looks up at me and smiles. Suddenly, all the air is sucked from the room; it must have been, because I can't catch my breath. He's gorgeous; he's fit; he's in my house, and I can't bloody speak to him.

Any minute now, he's going to find that out, and he'll retreat with an awkward excuse about having something else to do. I mean, I'm absolutely certain he must have something far more interesting and exciting to do than trying to hold a conversation with a neighbour who can't reply.

"So this is your house huh?" Zak doesn't seem to have noticed I haven't spoken yet as he walks further into my home. "It's nothing like ours, is it? It's a lot bigger, for starters. Not that my mom and I need much space, y'know. It's still bigger than the last apartment we had in San Diego, and even after one day I know the neighbourhood is better." He winks at me as if he is including me in this analogy. "At least I have my own room now, with a real bed instead of a couch." He moves towards the kitchen with Zen jumping at his heels.

I don't remember inviting him in—maybe because I haven't said a word yet? But still, he shouldn't just assume. My eyes follow his progress through to the kitchen, but my feet stubbornly refuse to move.

"Oh my god, your kitchen is awesome!" he exclaims as if I've followed him. "Do you cook? You must cook—you've got, like, fifty different pans. Holy crap, you have one of those refrigerators that dispenses ice. We had one of those at home, and I asked Mom if we could get one here. She told me it was either have an ice dispenser or eat next month, and I figured eating was kinda more important."

When I finally manage to uproot my feet from the entrance hall carpet and follow him, he's already sitting at my breakfast bench, draping his slim body across it and regarding me with bright eyes and an even brighter smile. His long, slender fingers are linked together, and he flicks his eyebrows at me in greeting.

"I've been working in the garden all morning, and it's hotter than an oven out there. I didn't think it got so hot in the UK. Mom kicked me out of the house because I was getting in her way, and I guess she needs to organise more than I need to unpack everything at once like it's Christmas. I got a little carried away." He snorts then sits up and points to the bottle I still have in my hand. "So, are you gonna offer me one of those beers?"

I frown. He's getting a bit ahead of himself, isn't he? Plus he doesn't look old enough to even be thinking about drinking beer.

"H-how old are y-y…?"

"How old?" He laughs in apparent delight. "I'm twenty-three, dude. Drinking age is eighteen here, right? Do I look younger than that?" He shakes his head, his blonde hair falling over his eyes. He blows it away. "I guess I must, because I get ID'd all the time. You can see my driver's licence if you want, except it's on the table in my hall."

I purse my lips and narrow my eyes as he regards me with an earnest expression.

"You don't believe me?" He gives an exaggerated gasp, as if he's taken my frown as a challenge. I find myself smirking at his shamelessness, unable to meet his eye for long without blushing.

His eyes are so blue. They make my dull, brown eyes seem inadequate by comparison.

He still hasn't noticed I have yet to speak a full sentence in his presence. Is that because he doesn't care? Or is it because he usually talks so much he's used to everyone else not being able to get a word in? While *I* might not have spoken a full sentence, I don't think he's taken a breath between his. Every thought in his head seems to come out of his mouth without any sort of verbal filter.

I reach into the refrigerator for a beer and hand it to him.

"Thanks, er, Niall."

I gasp and stare at him with wide eyes. *How the hell...?*

"I n-n-never t-t-told y-y-you..."

He grimaces and bites his lip. "Sorry, I'm not psychic, I swear. I didn't read your mind or anything creepy like that. Please don't freak out on me. I just assumed this was your mail." He indicates the pile of opened letters on the breakfast bench. "That's a nice name, Niall. I have a friend at school, he's called Neal. Do you think the names mean the same thing?"

"Sc-school?" I question, since he has just told me he's twenty-three.

"I meant *had* a friend, jeez." He rolls his eyes—at himself I think, not at me. "I left school five years ago. I went to college over in the States, but we call it school. I had to drop out, just before I graduated, for various reasons. So I need to enrol into a college here once everything's organised and stuff. Don't know if they run the same kind of courses. I guess I'm not fighting my case too well, saying I'm still at school when I'm trying to convince you I'm not underage, huh?" He jumps down from the stool and runs to the door. "I'll go get my driver's licence, then you'll know for sure you're not giving alcohol to a minor."

He's gone before I can stop him. I try to call him back, but I barely stutter past the first four 'N's of 'No need' and he's disappeared.

I look down at Zen in surprise. "Well, do you think he'll be back, Zen?" He tips his head to one side and gives a small whine, his eyebrows knitting together in confusion. He's wondering where his new friend has gone, while I'm feeling like I've been run over by a steamroller. *Phew!*

"Hey!"

I almost jump out of my skin when Zak returns less than a minute later and pops his head inside the kitchen before entering.

"Whoa, sorry." He snorts. "Didn't mean to startle you. Here." He thrusts the scruffiest looking California driving licence in front of my face. I have to move back in order to view it; even then it's a little blurred.

Giving him a self-conscious sideways glance, I pick up my glasses and place them on my nose. His licence comes into focus, and I see that he is indeed twenty-three. His former address was in San Diego. He's already told me some of the reasons for him coming over here. I doubt I'll get the opportunity to hear the full story.

"Nice!" Zak comments, pointing at my glasses. "I have to wear glasses too, but only for distance and driving. I guess it comes with age."

I frown, and he gasps and shakes his head.

"Oh, shit, no, I didn't mean you. I meant me. That wasn't a dig at your age, Niall. That's a really nice name, did I say that already? I guess it's safe to assume you're a little older than me, since you got some grey goin' on there." He indicates my temples and the silvery streaks that have been developing over the last few years. They show up more in dark hair, unfortunately. My hand moves to my temple to smooth over the silver. His fingers wave close enough for me to feel the rush of air they create. "Don't cover it up. It's kinda cute, and dignified. How old are you, Niall? If you don't mind me asking?"

Oh god, a direct question, although it took him longer than most people to get to this stage. I feel my heartbeat speeding up, and my breathing becomes shallower in panic. What am I supposed to do now? I try to splutter it out, to no avail. I'm stuck on the 'F' like a broken record and holding onto the bench for support.

"Shit, Niall, you don't have to answer. I'm just being nosey, so don't sweat it. You could just write it down if you want, or I could guess, and you can nod if I'm right. Makes no difference to me." His words are casual, but it's his smile that blows me away: so concerned, so gentle. That simple action changed his whole demeanour. He's far more mature than was my initial impression. "But just so you know, Niall." He continues as I try to concentrate on not blushing furiously. "I heard you talking to Zen just before, and you have a really nice voice, just like your name. Niall."

Okay, how many times has he said my name in the last twenty seconds? He'll wear it out. It sounds nice when he says it, though, and when he elongates the vowels it starts sounding a *bit too* nice. I'm too caught up in that to worry how unusual it is for someone to just accept that I have trouble speaking and not think I am a complete freak.

I write down my age. I am twenty years older than him. Gosh! That's a sobering thought. I mean, I'd assumed he was younger, and it was a relief to find out he is actually over eighteen, but still. There's a bit of an age gap, isn't there? It doesn't stop me looking; it just stops me acting on any kind of attraction. That's all.

"Forty-three!" Zak reads over my shoulder, and I see from the corner of my eye that he is nodding. "Cool. Although I gotta say, you don't look forty-three, Niall. More like thirty, really."

Is it my imagination, or do I detect a hint of disappointment in his tone? Why would that be? I turn to look directly at him but he won't meet my eye, although it's not surprising, because he towers above me when he's standing this close. I'm five foot nine, and I've never felt so dwarfed. He must be six foot at least.

He thought I was younger? I don't think I look younger. I'm not exactly craggy, but as Zak pointed out, I do have a few grey hairs dotted about my dark head.

"So, are you gonna show me around?" he asks quickly, a light blush on his cheeks as if he's revealed something he didn't want to, and now he's embarrassed and trying to distract by changing the subject. I have no idea why.

I think he's being a bit pushy, and forward, but he's here and doesn't seem to give a shit about my stutter. I haven't yet managed to string two words together and he hasn't batted an eye. That's a refreshing change, and he doesn't appear to think I'm being rude—which I'm not, but a lot of people assume I am—when I just grunt an answer.

He seemed interested in my garden before, so we'll start there and see how long this lasts. I indicate that he should follow, and he grins, taking my hint, with Zen jumping about his feet as we go outside.

"We've never had a garden before," Zak tells me as he inspects the seedlings I've just transferred to my flower beds. "I'm looking forward to getting stuck into this one. I think I'll need to do some research on what to grow in an English garden. Hey, maybe you could help me. You seem to know what you're doing. Mom says I can pretty much do what I want. Personally, I think she's saying that to keep me around." He twists his mouth as he stands to look towards the fence separating his garden and mine. "I'd never leave her to do this on her own." He whispers so quietly I don't think I was meant to hear, but I did.

I feel my breath catch as his entire demeanour changes again. He suddenly seems to have the weight of the world on his shoulders, and it ages him, making him look far older than his years and actions would suggest.

"I've stayed too long." He turns to me, and the smile is back on his face, but not in his eyes. He downs the last of his beer and holds the bottle up in salute. "Thanks for the beer, Niall, but I gotta go. Should I put this in your recycling?" I nod and smile, feeling strangely less self-conscious than I usually do when I can't reply. "Cool."

Zen jumps around Zak's feet as we move to the front door. He chuckles at my dog's antics and crouches down to give him a farewell scratch.

"Hey, buddy, I'll see ya again. I'm just next door. Anytime you wanna escape under the fence feel free to come over."

He stands again and winks at me as he does. "Invitation's open to you too, Niall, although I doubt you'd fit under the fence." He snorts as I raise an eyebrow in amusement. "See ya, Niall. Thanks for showing me around."

He's gone before I can tell him it was no problem. I think he probably guessed that much anyway.

Well, there's a first. I think Zen and I may have made a new friend. I feel like I've been hit by a hurricane. My new neighbour's a bit of a whirlwind.

Chapter 3

In which Zen adopts my new neighbour

O VER THE NEXT few weeks, Zen takes Zak's word as gospel and pushes under the fence at every opportunity in order to visit his newfound friend. This inevitably pushes his newfound friend into visiting me in order to return my errant dog to his rightful owner. As a consequence, I have spent quite a bit of time in Zak's company.

"I think he thinks we're his second home." Zak chuckles as he hands Zen over for the second time today.

"C-come in f-for c-coffee?" I ask. Zak's broad smile is the only reason I even attempt the question.

"Mom says I shouldn't bother you. I'm just returning Zen to you. I'm not bothering you, am I?"

"N-not b-bothering me in the slightest, Zak, really."

He isn't. He breezes in with Zen tucked under his arm and fills my house with noise. It isn't unwelcome. If I'd been asked six weeks ago, I would have given an absolute 'no' to having any kind of regular visit from a neighbour. Now, I can't imagine not having him here every day.

Zen is still jumping about Zak's heels and demanding more attention. I roll my eyes at his brazenness.

"I a-apologise for my s-slut of a m-mutt." I smile at Zak's snort. "I c-could b-block the hole in the fence."

"Don't you dare." Zak looks up, horrified. For a moment, I am struck by how sharply he says this but don't have time to wonder why, because Zak continues talking at his usual breakneck speed. "Zen's kinda cute when he turns up on our deck with his nose pressed to the glass of our French doors, wagging his sweet, stumpy little tail. He makes me laugh, y'know? Reminds me of the dog I had when I was a kid." He scratches Zen's stomach hoping—I think—that I don't see his sad expression.

Zak talks constantly, but always I feel I'm not getting the whole story. He has plenty to say about his life in Southern California. He shares funny stories about his friends and their antics, interspersed with a little homesickness. He talks about what he likes to do and his plans for the future, but there is a distinct lack of information about his family, specifically his dad.

All I know is that his dad died and had no family, so that's why Zak's mum wanted to move back to England to be close to hers. Zak says he was happy to come, but I wonder what it means for him to leave all the places behind that remind him of his father. He never talks about that, and I'm a little afraid to ask. Beneath his cheery, chatty, confident exterior, I think there is quite a fragile young man keeping it together for the sake of his grieving mother. But Zak is grieving too. I can see it in his eyes every time he stops himself from talking about his dad.

So, yes, I want to ask, but I don't—and not because it would take me forever to stutter through the questions—because I'm afraid if I do he might break.

I'm sure he'll tell me in his own time, someday.

Zak and Zen have quickly become firm friends. Zen seems to just go gaga over him. It's funny, really. I mean, Zen is my dog, but I know for a fact if I handed him over to Zak right now he wouldn't even give me a second thought. It's like they're soul mates. Zen sits with him on the sofa, which was an honour only reserved for me before Zak came along. The funniest thing is Zen isn't really that friendly a dog. He's always been quite protective of me and wary of strangers—all except Zak, that is.

So Zen escapes to Zak's house whenever his canine whim takes him; Zak brings him back and stays to talk. It's quickly become routine. I don't really mind. It's a bit of a novelty having someone visit who actually wants to be here, and Zak's constant, unconditional chatter is quite refreshing.

I guess he needs someone to listen, and I'm the nearest ear and someone who conveniently can't tell him to shut up. Well, I could, but it would take me all day.

He talks when I'm relaxing in the living room. He talks when I'm busy in the kitchen. He follows me around the house if I'm cleaning. He even helps, which means the jobs get done quicker. I don't ask him to; I just stuck a cloth and some polish in his hands one day, and he started dusting without breaking his flow.

He doesn't seem to have any problem with the fact that I sometimes don't say a word. I think he knows if I say anything at all, it's important, because it takes me so damn long I usually don't bother. At those times, he always listens, never tries to hurry me and never puts words in my mouth. He just waits, as if what I'm saying is the only thing in the world that matters. I'm sure that's just my perception of it, though. He waits because he's polite and patient, and he probably doesn't have anything better to do.

I suppose what I'm saying is that I enjoy his company, even though I know he's really just here for Zen.

"You're like one of those Ents in *Lord of the Rings*, Niall," he jokes as I hand him his coffee having given up trying to ask about his day because I couldn't get past the 'H' in 'How'. When I scowl and turn away, he laughs and grabs my arm. "No, I don't mean because you look old and craggy like a tree, because you really don't." I know what he meant, I've read *Lord of the Rings*. "I mean because Ents never say anything unless it's worth taking a long time to say it. They take all morning just to say 'hello'."

I still take offence, and then I want to laugh at the way he tries to backtrack and sticks his foot even further in his mouth. I eventually put him out of his misery and tell him it's okay—taking about ten minutes to say it.

"H-how is y-your m-m-mum?" I ask out of politeness, and because sometimes I feel a little guilty that he does all the talking.

I've yet to meet his mum. I know her name is Rachel, and she's waved to me from a distance, but I always manage to duck inside the house before there's any danger of her making her way across the drive to talk to me. She probably thinks I'm a right grumpy bastard. I haven't even looked at her long enough to be able to describe her. How neighbourly is that, for god's sake? Not for the first time, I think I may have turned into a bit of a recluse.

Zen jumps about Zak's feet for attention, and Zak absently scratches at the dog's ears before settling on a stool at my breakfast bench and replying to my enquiry.

"Mom's okay, I guess." His usual lengthy response to any of my questions is not forthcoming, and it distracts me from my own thoughts. I regard him as he draws circles on my bench with his forefinger. He looks unhappy.

I sit down beside him at the bench and try to meet his eye.

"T-tell m-me," I urge, wondering if he's ready to open up a little more, or just share something about the grief he's feeling but obviously can't show at home because he doesn't want to upset his mum.

He smiles, laughing softly, then shrugs.

"I don't know, Niall. She always seems to get so pissed off with me. She tells me I should be out trying to make friends. What am I, six? I can hardly go to the play park and pick up a few best buddies, can I? I'd get arrested." He rolls his eyes, and I can't help laughing. He grimaces as he continues. "We had a fight last night, about how I should get out more and not spend so much time…" He stops himself. He does occasionally put his verbal filters in place, but I think he may have been about to say his mother thinks he comes over here too much.

"Mom wants me to help her and my aunt with their business, so I've been driving all over the place for them." He looks thoroughly fed up. "Yesterday, I drove a two-hundred-mile round trip to pick up a catering refrigerator for her and then she gets mad at me for falling asleep on the sofa after dinner and not doing the dishes. I'm twenty-three not sixteen.

"I wasn't lazing about, shirking my responsibilities like a teenager. I was tired after doing her a favour. And then I wish I could have just stayed in the States, but I feel guilty, because how could she have done this without me? She would've stayed if I'd said I wanted to, but she needed to be near her sister.

"My dad had no family, and I had no ties. No massive ones, anyway, so we weren't really leaving anyone behind—just a few friends, and we keep in touch over the Net. It's not like we can't speak anytime we want." Zak shrugs, a distant look in his eyes and I wonder who he has left behind.

"She just never seems happy, y'know," he continues. "I got it in the neck for not mowing the lawn this morning. I was gonna do it, but she just cussed me out before I could make a start. Then she said I should go and find a job. I can't get a job and work for her at the same time, although if I got a job, I would at least get paid, and then I'd have some money so I could go out and meet other people. But then she'd probably be pissed that I wasn't available to do all her dirty work."

Sometimes I want to stop him and make him take a breath.

It takes me a few moments to register everything he's told me, because sometimes it's like getting all the information at once in a zip file. If I understand correctly, he's being taken for granted at home, and I feel his frustration. If his mum could hear just how supportive he is of her, she'd appreciate how much he has given up to be here with her. For her, it isn't so much a new start as a return home. For him, it is a complete change of lifestyle, not to mention the culture shock.

"Y-you're n-not doing too much, are you, Zak?"

He looks at me as if I've said something amazing then puts his arm around me and hugs me to him.

"Nah!" He releases his hold, but my brain has gone to mush at how amazing that felt. "I'm just whinin', Niall. Mom was having a bad day, I guess. It's understandable, isn't it? She lost her husband. We've moved halfway around the world. She's bound to find it hard to adjust."

I'm trying to process how good it felt to have his body pressed against mine, however brief it was. I've been too long starved of physical contact. I need to control myself. I'm not really thinking about what I'm saying when I reply.

"Y-y-you l-lost your d-dad, Zak. You moved to another country too. Sh-she should cut you s-some slack."

"Mom cuts me enough slack, Niall." He looks up, his eyes flashing in anger. I take a step back, holding up my hands in submission and apology. He hangs his head with a sigh. "No need to apologise, dude. I'm sorry I snapped." He looks up again and smiles. "Hey, can I hang out here for a little longer? Mom's still on the warpath about the lawn, and I'm feeling rebellious."

I laugh. I don't mind him being here, although I'm a little worried he's using me as an excuse to avoid responsibilities. I don't want to get on Rachel's bad side if his being here causes conflict between them.

I suppose I shouldn't really complain, since over the last few weeks I've enjoyed getting to know him. I even look forward to his visits. Does that sound a little sad and lonely? I didn't think I *was* lonely until he blasted into my life. I had Zen, and he and I were doing okay. I really didn't think I needed anything or anyone else in my life.

'Set in my ways' is how, I suppose, I would describe myself. I'd become a creature of routine and habit. Zak came along and has broken it all to pieces, but not in a bad way. I suppose I should just enjoy his company while I can. I don't think it will be for very much longer. He's only been here a month; once he finds his feet, makes some new friends and spreads his wings, he won't need me: the grumpy old sod who lives next door.

"So can I stay?" He's waiting for me to say yes, and it's never seemed so important to him before. I mean, he invited himself into my house the first time he came around. He never waited for my approval then; nor has he since, until now.

He's looking at me with great anticipation on his face, and I am suddenly struck by just how lovely he is, like I'm seeing him clearly for the first time. His skin is perfect: smooth and tanned, with a hint of freckles, and there's always a slight flush to his cheeks—I think—because he talks so much he overheats.

I realise I've taken too long to answer when Zak gets up to leave.

"Hey, Niall, if you don't want me to stay I can go. I don't mind, just, I can't go home right now. Mom's too angry. I can go to a movie or something. I'm cool with that."

"On your own?" I gasp, too shocked to stutter.

He stops on his way to the door and gives me a curious look.

"I don't mind going on my own. I've done it plenty of times." He tips his head to one side and grins. "Of course, I don't have to be on my own, if you come with me."

"W-what?" I swallow. That wasn't why I commented. I wasn't fishing for him to ask me. I was actually about to tell him he was welcome to stay here.

"Sure, Niall, come with me to the movies." His usual confident tone has been replaced by a slight nervousness, and he bites his lower lip as he waits for me to answer. "Why not?"

Why not? Can he hear himself? He's asking me to go to the movies with him like a date. I'm twenty years older than him. Doesn't he see it's not the thing to do?

I look at his eager expression. Maybe he doesn't. Maybe he isn't even seeing this as a date, since he's looking for someone to hang out with, *not* someone to go out with. He doesn't have any friends, he told me; he hasn't had any time to find any. Does he count me as a friend? That feels good, and certainly more appropriate than what was going through my head when he hugged me before.

"O-okay." I nod.

"Oh boy, that's great, Niall. You can drive, since I don't have a car yet, and I don't think Mom will let me drive hers after our fight. What are we going to see? Let's get the listings up on my cell and see what's on. Can I log onto your wi-fi? Or maybe we could just turn up and see what we can get tickets for. Should we eat first? Or maybe we could go for something to eat after. What are the best places near here? That's always supposing you can cope with my stomach rumbling all through the movie."

Oh my god, I can't hear myself think. With him still rambling on about the order in which we are going to do this, I grab my jacket and my keys and then him. He's still talking as I drag him out of the door.

Chapter 4

In which I go to the movies with my new neighbour

S o THERE'S THIS guy I went to college with in the States, that says he knows the guy who trains with the guy who was stunt coordinator for this movie," Zak whispers to me as we settle in our seats ready to watch.

So far, he hasn't taken a breath since we left the house. He talked right through dinner—where he fit in any time to actually eat I don't know, but suddenly his plate was empty. Is he going to talk through the entire movie? He does when we're at home, but then we hadn't paid especially to see those movies, and he does usually have some pretty funny stuff to say about what we're watching.

I put on my 3D glasses and then sort out my popcorn and small drink. Zak juggles with a hot dog, nachos and a huge, bucket-sized soft drink. He also has popcorn. How can someone eat so much in one go? And after I've just watched him eat enough pizza to sink a battleship. He's skinny as a rake, too, although, admittedly a lot of that is muscle, so he isn't so much skinny as wiry, and firm. I need to stop looking now!

"S-sure y-you've got enough to eat there, Zak?" I point at his food trays by way of a distraction.

"Just about." He smirks—an action that provides its own set of distractions.

"N-no wonder your mum k-kicked you out t-tonight. Probably saved her a fortune in food shopping." I remark as he begins to eat his hot dog. He snorts.

"Shit, Niall, I'd tell you to be quiet because the movie's about to start but that's the most I've heard you say in one go. It only took you four weeks, three days, two hours and—" he looks at his watch "—three and a half minutes."

I take a handful of popcorn and shove it in his mouth before he can say anything else.

"S-sarcastic bugger. Shut up!" I tell him as he snorts with delighted laughter. "The movie's about to start."

Chapter 5

In which I discover I've made a friend

ABOUT A WEEK after our cinema trip, I'm unloading my shopping—all four bags of it, most of it dog food and, for some reason, stuff Zak likes that he added to the bottom of my shopping list, cheeky bugger—when I am faced with my worst nightmare: a neighbour actually speaking to me. Or rather, a neighbour that isn't Zak.

"It's Niall, isn't it?"

Oh god. Who's this random woman talking to me on the street? I don't lift my head, or turn in her direction.

"Hmm!" I grunt as I heave the oversize bag of dog food out of the boot of the car. Zen might be a small dog but he has a hell of an appetite.

"I'm Rachel, Zak's mother."

Oh! I actually look up and make eye contact. I recognise her now.

"H-h-hello!" I try to smile politely whilst I struggle over a word that most people would have already spoken without even thinking about it.

Rachel is nothing like Zak. She's tiny. Her dark hair is arranged in a neat bun at the back of her head, and her eyes are a light brown, almost hazel, with a slight twinkle as they search mine. Well, okay, that might be a bit like Zak. But Rachel doesn't even have an accent, despite having lived in the States for at least twenty-three years that I know about. There might be a slight drawl there, but nothing as strong as Zak's.

"Zak's told me all about you, Niall, and of course I've already met Zen." She looks up at the house, where we she can no doubt hear said Zen going crackers because I haven't opened the door yet. She looks back at me, and her eyes crinkle as she smiles. There's the resemblance—that grin. Zak must get his fair complexion from his dad, I presume, but he gets his smile from his mum.

What did she say? Zak's told her about me. Oh hell!

"I h-h-hope it w-was all g-g-g…" I get stuck and shrug in embarrassment. I take a deep breath to try again but Rachel interrupts me.

"Oh yes, it was all good, although he never mentioned that you…" She clears her throat awkwardly, biting her lip and looking away.

Was she going to point out my stutter? Like I hadn't noticed I sound like a vinyl record with the needle stuck? And how can Zak have told her *all* about me and not have mentioned the most prominent fact about me?

Oh shit, now she's giving me the look—all sympathetic and trying for understanding but only managing mild pity. She probably thinks I'm some sort of headcase. I know she's already told Zak he spends too much time with me. Zak stopped short of saying it, but I'm almost certain that's what he was going to say.

"Well, it's nice to finally meet you, Niall, and I apologise that it's taken me so long to actually come over and speak to you, but you know how it is. Moving house can be busy enough, but we moved from another country too." She smiles—a more genuine, less awkward smile this time—but there is still a hint of pity in her eyes.

I hate that. I hate it with a passion. This is why I don't bloody speak to neighbours, people, anyone.

"I hope you don't mind Zak spending so much time over at your place. He's gaga over your dog. Is that Zen I can hear barking?"

I nod, since that doesn't require a verbal answer, and she doesn't give me a chance to answer anyway as she launches into another monologue.

"It's such a relief to have a nice neighbour. You worry about things like that when you move into a new community, but everyone in the street is really nice, and you've been such a good friend to Zak. Thank you."

"Y-you're w-welcome." She doesn't even sound a little unhappy about Zak's seeming obsession with my dog and my house.

She thinks I've been a good friend. I hadn't even seen it that way. He burst into my life, and he's constantly there. I always thought his visits would taper off once he found some new friends, but here we are, just over a month in, and that hasn't happened yet.

"Zen is so super cute, I don't mind him coming round at all," Rachel continues. Zak obviously gets his skill for talking nonstop from his mother. I've got shopping to unload. There's not a lot, but some of it is frozen, and it's a hot day. "You can visit anytime too, Niall. Just pop over for a coffee and a chat. I feel so bad that we've been here five weeks and we only just met now. I've been super busy, and I guess Zak's been doing the neighbourly thing pretty well. I worried that he wouldn't make any friends. He certainly seems to have found a friend in Zen."

That's what she meant when she referred to friendship, although that's a bit sad, isn't it, that she thinks Zak's made a friend even though it's only a dog?

"Zen seems t-to h-have c-claimed Zak as his." I nod and smile. "It w-was n-nice m-meeting you, er…"

"Rachel!" She chuckles, and I think she may have thought I'd forgotten her name, rather than the real reason for the hesitation, which is that new names are particularly difficult for me. Except Zak's. I never seem to have had a problem with his name.

I pick up two of my bags and turn, hoping Rachel will take this as a sign the conversation might be winding down. Saying goodbye can sometimes take me an age, so I rely on people picking up my non-verbal cues. Zak does it so well, but Rachel doesn't take the hint. She doesn't appear to think I'm being sullen or grumpy when I turn my back, however. This is another trait she shares with Zak. At least I'm not running away from her. That's a positive. I suppose I should make an effort to get to know her; she is Zak's mother, after all.

"We weren't so lucky with neighbours where we were living before." She takes my other two bags of shopping and follows me to my door.

God, is she going to be like her son and invite herself in? I can just about cope with Zak; I'm not sure I can cope with his mum invading my space as well.

"They were noisy and interfering," Rachel continues. "Unfortunately, we happened to choose the most homophobic apartment block in the whole of San Diego. We had to wait such a long time until they granted Zak a British passport for his dual nationality. We were there six months, and Zak went through hell because of some of the assholes in that block. It was awful for him, and we wouldn't even have moved, but we got such a great offer on the house, way above the asking price, we had to take it. I feel so guilty about it all, but we couldn't know really, until we actually got there, and the stuff started."

Was Zak a victim of homophobia? Is that what she's telling me? Is he gay? How has he never managed to divulge that snippet of information? Did he get beaten up for it? Is that why? Is that the real reason he hasn't made any friends over here? Is he just being cautious?

I could introduce him to some of my friends, although I tend to keep them all at arm's length since a lot of them took the side of my ex when we broke up. A lot of them are still in touch with him, and I don't want to move in the same circles as him. I definitely wouldn't want to subject Zak to my ex-boyfriend's spiteful vindictiveness.

I realise Rachel is staring at me. She has a look of concern on her face but I think it's concern for Zak, not for the fact that I zoned out. After what she's just told me, I wouldn't blame her. This neighbourhood has always been very accepting.

"Zak is gay?" I just need to check, so I'm not making assumptions here. I still cannot believe, after all the talking Zak has done over the last five weeks, he hasn't mentioned this once.

Rachel nods and grimaces. "Oh god, that's not a problem here, is it? Maybe I shouldn't have said, if he hasn't told you himself. He was out in the States, not that it did him any good. I felt so helpless about the whole thing. We decided he would play it safe until we'd tested the waters here. Everyone is really friendly, but you never really know how someone is going to react. If his dad had been alive…" She stops and heaves a sigh, looking unhappy and a little shaky and emotional.

I guess if Zak's father had been alive, then they would all still be living in the States, and we would never have met. It's awful they've both been worried about coming out over here. It's awful that Zak hasn't felt he could tell me.

"Zak is s-safe h-here, R-Rachel. I-I'll look after h-him," I assure her, placing a hand on her arm. "I-I've n-never had any trouble h-here in s-sixteen years."

What the hell? Why in a million years would she be expecting me to say that? I've effectively outed myself and managed to make it sound completely creepy at the same time. I might as well have told her I was inviting Zak to come and look at some puppies. Now she probably thinks I'm some sort of predator, preying on vulnerable, young men.

When I finally make eye contact again, I realise she doesn't look shocked at all. She looks relieved. She reaches out and touches my arm, her eyes quite moist with emotion. She leans in and gives me a kiss on the cheek.

"Oh, Niall. Zak said you were a sweetie. Thank you so much."

"No problem." I don't even stammer I'm so taken aback by her reaction.

"Well, I gotta go." She snaps out of her pensive mood and is suddenly bright and breezy. "I'm catering for a wedding at the weekend, and I have one hundred and fifty individual cupcakes to ice before Friday. I'll see you around, Niall. Come over anytime, although come to the front door, I don't think you'll manage to fit under the fence the way Zen does." She giggles as she waves goodbye and walks across to her drive.

As I watch her disappear through her front door, I feel a bit like I've been swept away by a tsunami. She and Zak might look nothing like each other but they could both compete for England when it comes to talking. I wish I could be a fly on the wall in that house when they get started. It must be noisy. Do I really want to take her up on the offer of coffee? I might not have any ears left, because they'll both have talked them off.

Chapter 6

*In which Zak is quite chivalrous
and I'm a little sarcastic*

I HEAR YOU SPOKE to Mom," Zak mentions as he enters the house later that evening and takes up his usual position on the kitchen bench.

"Y-yes, although she spoke, I listened."

Zak rolls his eyes in embarrassment, which makes me laugh.

"Yeah, my mom can talk up a storm."

I raise my eyebrows and regard him over the top of my glasses. He snorts.

"Yeah, okay, I know I can talk too, but Mom holds the record. Where do you think I acquired the skill?"

"You m-mean you actually stopped t-to listen f-for a moment so you could learn something?"

"Hey, less of the sarcasm, mister. I know stuff. I know when to stop and listen."

This time, *I* roll my eyes, and he chuckles before jumping down and making more of a fuss of Zen.

For a moment I watch them both with a smile on my face, but I mostly watch Zak. I am absolutely certain he is using Zen as a reason to avoid my next question, which I am sure he knows I'm going to ask.

"Why didn't you tell me you're gay?" I tip my head to one side.

He looks up at me with a startled expression before quickly recovering as he stands, thrusting his hands in his pockets.

"Why didn't you tell me you're gay?" He raises his eyebrows as I narrow mine.

"I h-have an excuse. It would h-have taken me all d-d-day. G's and H's are n-nasty," I point out, emphasising a stutter as I do. "Y-you t-talk constantly, yet y-you never t-told me you're gay. That n-never came up, not once."

He shrugs and shuffles his feet uncomfortably. He looks unhappy, or maybe he looks uncertain; that's a better way of putting it. But why? Does he think I'm angry with him? Lord knows, I understand why he didn't tell me.

"Your mum told me about the trouble you had where you lived before you came here."

Again Zak shrugs as if it's a minor problem. but I see the pain that flashes across his face. It lingers in his eyes and joins other hurt and pain that runs deeper than just the trouble he had with homophobes.

There are other things Zak never talks to me about, and one of them is his dad. He mentioned he doesn't talk about him at home because it upsets his mum, but in five weeks, he has only mentioned the man twice. Is he just taking time to open up? Does he need an assurance that I'll listen? He surely knows that I will. I'm hard-pressed to get a word in some days.

"Y-you know if you e-ever want to talk about anything, Zak, I'm here," I offer. He doesn't appear to have anyone else.

I know he'll find his own circle of friends eventually, but until then I'll be here for him while he needs me.

Zak heaves a sigh, and it's a shaky sigh; I guess his emotions are as raw as his mother's are right now. I wonder if his being here, and talking nonstop is a coping mechanism.

"Thanks, Niall," he replies after what seems like an abnormal length of silence for him.

I pat his arm and nod as I walk away to put the kettle on.

Zak resumes the fuss he was making over Zen. Sometimes I think he uses Zen as an excuse not to look at me or to avoid sensitive subjects. Or maybe he's using Zen as a comfort blanket. Either way, he and Zen both seem to benefit from the contact.

"So, are we taking Niall out for a walk tonight, Zen?" I hear Zak stage-whisper to my dog.

I groan, because Zak knows by now that when that word is mentioned in Zen's presence the dog goes mental. He is currently running around in circles, yapping and jumping in excitement.

And what did he mean, taking Niall out for a walk? Huh! I could take offence at that, but then Zak smiles at me, and Zen jumps about my heels. Both of them regard me with those puppy-dog eyes that I can't resist, and I just shake my head and laugh.

"Come on, Zen," Zak calls as he jumps up and runs out of the kitchen. "Let's get ready, buddy." He glances back at me with another one of those smiles, and I feel my breath catch in my throat.

I remember what Rachel said and what I promised her. I really do want to protect him, but as what? His friend? His neighbour? I can't surely be anything more than that, can I? Knowing he's gay for definite opens up certain possibilities, but our age gap is a barrier, surely, and anyway, Rachel didn't mean that kind of protection, did she?

"Hey, Niall, come on. We're getting a bit impatient out here, dude," Zak calls from the hall, jerking me out of my daydream.

"Huh, I was about to make some coffee." I huff.

As I emerge from the kitchen, I stop in mid-grouch. Zak is holding my jacket out to me, his smile as bright as ever. I slide my arms in, and he settles it on my shoulders, smoothing it down for me. That's…well…very unexpected and chivalrous.

"Th-thank you." I smile up at him, and he regards me, biting his lip as if he has something to say.

He's still smoothing down the sleeve of my jacket, which is making my arm tingle now. He flicks a piece of dust from the fabric, brushing it to remove any remnants.

"You know, you're not the only one who can listen, Niall, right?" He looks like he's—oh, he is! He's blushing. Oh! He searches my face waiting for me to respond, his cheeks coloured with the loveliest blush I've ever seen. "I always have time if you need someone to talk to."

I am overwhelmed by feelings I just can't process. What did I ever do to deserve such an amazing neighbour? He is always so patient, past the point where others might have given up and finished the sentence for me. He's just a lovely young man.

I smile and nod, patting his arm as I move past him to get to the door.

"I kn-know you do. Th-thanks."

Chapter 7

In which Zak assumes I am an axe murderer

H OW COME YOU live in this big house all on your own, Niall?"
Zak is currently perched on my kitchen bench, swinging his
legs like a kid, except his legs are almost long enough to reach
the ground, and they are quite a bit more hairy than a child's
legs might be in the long beach shorts he's wearing. They're also
quite well defined, muscle-wise. He's barefoot too. His feet, like
his hands, are slender and elegant. It's all very distracting.

I try to focus on cooking dinner without burning anything.

"N-not always on my own," I finally manage to reply to his
query.

It isn't often he asks me a direct question like that. It's not that
he isn't curious; he just has other ways of getting the information
from me. This time, he took me by surprise. I need time to
formulate an answer.

"Did you live with someone?" His eyes are alive with curiosity.

"Yeah." I deliberately don't meet his eye, concentrating on my
sauce even though it doesn't need such close attention.

I knew this would come up eventually, and he can't exactly
do any detective work because I don't keep any photographs or
evidence of my previous partner anywhere that Zak has access to.

"So, was it a guy, or a girl?" Zak helps himself to some
chocolate raisins from a bowl on the bench beside him, as if he's
at the movies. He doesn't seem to think the question is in any way
unusual. Why would he ask that?

"G-guy," I reply, wrinkling my nose, still extremely interested in my sauce. "You know I'm gay." I can feel the tips of my ears getting very hot.

"Well, I didn't wanna make assumptions here, Niall. Maybe you just came out, and the girl left because you did, or maybe you're bi. I don't know."

"I'm not bi. I lived with a man for ten years. His name was G-Greg."

"What happened?" Zak pops another handful of raisins in his mouth, not fazed in the least to hear how long I was with my ex. His tone has changed, though; it's less curious and more gentle, or is that my imagination? "Did he leave? Was he an asshole and you kicked him out? Did he have an affair? Did you have an affair? Did you murder him and bury him underneath the patio? What?"

"No, I did not murder him!" I laugh at the outrageous statement, certain now that I imagined the change in his tone. Zak shrugs.

"I don't know that. This is England. You hear about these things happening all the time. Some mild-mannered, gentle soul takes too much crap, and they eventually snap and murder their partner. Maybe he was an abusive pisshead, and you brained him with the iron one night. Or maybe you hacked him to pieces with a blunt axe."

"Zak!" I chuckle helplessly. "You have been watching far too many soap operas and horror movies."

Zak jumps down from the bench and makes a fuss of Zen who is chilling in his basket.

"Hey, little buddy, you look completely wrecked."

He always knocks me sideways with his tendency to suddenly change the subject.

"You ran his legs off, I think." I smile down at them both, a little relieved the twenty questions about Greg have ceased. "He loves it when you take him out on a run."

Zak smiles back at me, and as always all of the air is sucked from the room. Fighting the need to grab hold of something for support because my knees have gone weak, I turn back to my sauce. It had better not get a damn lump in it, because I've never been so attentive of a cheese sauce before.

"So, tell me what happened to your ex-boyfriend, Niall."

Zak is standing right beside me now. Not invading my space—he never does—but he's close enough for me to think I could invade his if I wanted to. It makes my skin tingle. Thankfully, he's completely oblivious to the effect he has on me. I'm sure he wouldn't stand so close if he knew.

"W-what's t-to tell?" I reply to his demand. "H-he was an arse."

"So, you kicked him out?"

"He had an affair. It was the straw that broke the donkey's back," I explain.

"Affair?" The way he says the word I can tell he's outraged. He does seem the type to find infidelity unacceptable.

"That w-was one thing on the list."

"He sounds charming." Zak screws up his nose in disgust. "How long ago?"

"F-five years now."

"And you've been on your own all that time?" He sounds surprised, as if this is something that is somehow more outrageous than the fact someone was unfaithful. Why would he be so outraged?

"N-not on my own."

Why is he pushing this? He's never asked before now. Was he just looking for the right moment? I suppose if I'm expecting him to open up about his past, then I should tell him a little about mine, not that it is in any way interesting.

"So in those five years you've had boyfriends?" I shake my head because there's been no one since Greg. He left a wound that took a long time to heal and a scar that will probably be with me forever.

"No boyfriends."

"Girlfriends?" Zak continues to fish, and I screw up my nose and shake my head vigorously, frowning in bemusement. He shrugs and smirks. "Is that because you were afraid someone would get too close and discover the body underneath the patio?"

"Zak!" I laugh out loud, taking the towel I was wiping the bench with and flicking his leg with it. He yelps and leaps out of my reach, giggling. "I did not murder my ex-boyfriend. You are welcome to dig up the patio just to prove there isn't a body there."

"That doesn't prove anything, mister!" He places his hands on his hips and arches his eyebrows. "That just means you hid the body somewhere else." He flicks his eyebrows suggestively, and I laugh harder, my sides hurting. "I'll just have to tread carefully so I don't get the same treatment."

I click my tongue and shake my head in mock disgust, turning my attention back to the sauce, which is ready. I take it off the heat and take the macaroni to the sink to drain.

"Have you really been on your own for five years?" Zak is still stuck on this, and I have no idea why he finds it so fascinating. "Didn't you ever get lonely?"

"I was f-for a while but then I got Zen, and w-we're good." I look down at my sweet-natured Jack Russell, and he wags his little stump of a tail at the mention of his name.

Zen was my life-saver when I thought I couldn't bear another day of feeling so damn lonely, but I don't tell Zak this; he doesn't need to know how pathetic I was after Greg left.

Zak's questions seem to have come to an end, thankfully. He makes more fuss of my tired dog while I pour the cheese sauce over the macaroni, mix it and put it in the oven to finish it off.

Zak is muttering to Zen, and I sometimes get the impression he tells my dog things he would never tell anyone else, not even me. I guess his secrets are safe with Zen, though. It's not as if he could tell me what Zak whispers to him. Sometimes, like just now, I get the impression they are discussing me in depth. There are plenty of secrets Zen could tell about me, I'm certain.

Chapter 8

In which I would happily become an axe murderer

"Hey, Niall?" Zak calls from the entrance hall.

I've taken to leaving the front door unlocked whenever I discover Zen has made one of his escapes beneath the garden fence. I know it's never long before Zak appears, bringing my errant dog home.

"In the kitchen, making coffee!" I reply. I'd just decided to take a break. Zak's timing is perfect.

Zak is preceded into the kitchen by my wayward Jack Russell, who comes running in looking very smug. I chuckle.

"Hello, boy. Have you been for an extra walk today?"

"He turned up on our deck with a ball. How could I refuse?" Zak grins as he enters the kitchen. I grin back, holding up a mug as a question. He nods and takes up his usual perch on the bench beside me. "Oh, yes, please!"

Zak's phone rings, and he glances at the screen before groaning, jumping down off the bench and giving me an apologetic look.

"I'm really sorry, Niall, I have to take this." He grimaces. "I've been trying to get in touch with this asshole for weeks now."

"Oh, of c-course." I wave away his concerns, frowning as he retreats into the conservatory. He doesn't look or sound at all happy about whoever is trying to call him.

I take my coffee and wander back into my office with Zen at *my* heels for a change.

It's not long before my ears tune in to Zak's half of the conversation. It's not like I'm making an effort to eavesdrop; he isn't exactly being quiet.

"You were fucking him, Daniel, all the time we were together. How is that not cheating on me?" Zak shouts. "And it doesn't matter who told me. That's not the point really, is it? The point is you thought I wouldn't find out when I'm living halfway across the world? You know there is such a thing as Facebook over here as well? You changed your relationship status from single to in a relationship. Did you think I wouldn't see and work out who you were in a relationship with?"

There's a pause where I assume the guy Zak is shouting at is explaining himself, or backing himself into a corner, I don't know.

"I know it's none of my business now," he continues, sounding more upset than angry now. "But it was my business when you and I were still together, and you swore there wasn't anything going on between you and him. You're an asshole, Dan, you always were. I just deluded myself that you would change for me. I hope for his sake you'll change for him."

I hear the catch in his voice, and there's another pause. Zen gives me a quizzical look. With a quick hand gesture, I send my dog to Zak, since it sounds like he needs some canine support right now. If I could send Zen down the phone to bite this Daniel bloke on the arse I would happily do it.

Zak's whispered greeting of Zen is interrupted by his need to reply to what is becoming a rather heated discussion now.

"Yeah?" Zak snarls. "Well, I'm sorry you feel that way, Daniel fucking Masters, but I am the wronged party here." This pause hangs heavy, and is quickly followed by Zak's retort, "And fuck you too."

Well, that sounded very final.

Zak growls loudly in frustration, and I hear what I think is his phone being thrown down onto the wicker sofa in my conservatory. Zen yips, then Zak appears at my office door, looking a lot less cheerful and a lot more flushed than before.

"Everything okay?" I ask in concern.

Zak grimaces. "You heard, huh?"

I shrug in an attempt to allay his anxiety. I really hadn't meant to overhear. I'd just been worried about him. "I, er, wasn't listening."

Zak narrows his eyes, "The hell you weren't, Niall. You have listening down to a fine art. You'd get a gold medal if it was an Olympic event."

"Yeah, well, s-sorry." I am barely able to contain a snort. "I-I didn't m-mean to." Zak chuckles, the anger gone from his eyes.

"I'm not angry if you overheard. I'm just sorry you had to hear it at all. I had to speak to him. I've been getting his voicemail for days, and he eventually graced me with a live call so…" He shrugs, twisting his mouth awkwardly. "I needed the closure…if my language got bad, I'm sorry!"

"D-don't apologise." I try to reassure him I'm not offended in the least. His language was probably tame compared to the language I used when I kicked Greg out of my life.

"I've a good mind to call the other guy and fill him in on a few details, but I'm not that vindictive," Zak muses.

He sighs and leans against the door frame, picking at a hang nail on one of his slender fingers. I doubt he has a vindictive bone in his body, and the thought of someone cheating on him makes me feel sick. Oh my god, how could anyone ever do something like that to Zak? How could anyone ever think about being anything but completely faithful to him? I feel bad for him, because it's something I realise we have in common, and I wish we didn't. I know how much it can hurt.

I suddenly want to make it all better for him, but I just don't know how. I stand and join him in the doorway, laying a hand on his arm in sympathy.

"Is there anything I c-can do?"

He looks down at me and gives me a weak half-smile, shaking his head.

"No, not really. I always knew that guy was bad news, so it's my own fault. We split up just after mom sold our house. A lot of the trouble I had at the apartment was because of him, so his assholery isn't news to me really. People warned me about him when we first started dating, but I didn't listen. Maybe I should take some lessons in listening from you, huh?"

I chuckle, rubbing my thumb over the firm muscle of his forearm and trying not to react to the feel of his skin beneath my fingertips. I think I hear him catch his breath, but I'm not looking at his face so I can't see if he's noticed my inadvertent caress. God, I hope he hasn't. I got carried away there. I squeeze past him before I do anything more that might be construed as inappropriate.

"I-I'll make some t-tea." It's my excuse to get away from the temptation to wrap my arms around him and just hold him. That's not what he needs or what he wants from me.

A second later, Zak follows me, leaping across the hall to catch up.

"I think I'm beginning to like the English solution to everything, Niall." His bright smile is once more, firmly in place.

The English solution to everything is quite effective, especially when it can restore Zak's smile.

Chapter 9

*In which Zak seems to have lost his voice,
or maybe I've gone deaf*

Z AK IS STRANGELY quiet this evening as we walk Zen together.
The evening walk has quickly become a daily after-dinner
routine. However, his silence is definitely not routine.

Usually, he's talked the hind legs off a donkey by the time we
reach the end of the street. I swear he takes one breath in the
morning and another before he goes to bed—on a normal day,
that is—and I'm happy to listen, except he draws me out of myself
and listens to me as well. He has the patience of a saint, since I get
frustrated with myself, but he never shows any kind of irritation
when I get stuck on a word. He just waits, as if what I have to say
is the most important thing in the world.

Tonight, he remains quiet, pulling at leaves as we pass bushes
and throwing Zen's ball for him without so much as a grunt. Is
he sick? Has he talked so much he's given himself laryngitis?
Something is definitely not right.

"T-tell me w-what's wrong," I urge him gently.

He shrugs but doesn't look at me. He seems very unhappy
about something. I suppose I just have to wait until he's ready.

We walk through the park and around the lake, and Zak stops
to throw some stones into the water. Usually, he laughs at Zen,
who goes to jump in after them but then at the last minute thinks

better of it, because he's a little dog and it's a big lake. Not even Zen's antics are lifting my friend's spirits tonight. What can the matter be?

"I got a job," Zak eventually admits, as if this is some terrible confession he's been dreading telling me.

"Th-that's g-great," I say, because it is, isn't it? He should be happy. "Y-you w-wanted one, you s-said so."

"I know. I do want one, and I need the money to save up for a car, but it means I can't walk Zen during the day anymore."

Is that why he's unhappy? Because he can't walk Zen? It's not as if Zen is his responsibility. Oh, wait—does he think I'll be unhappy about it? I don't want him to feel obligated just because he's been doing it all these weeks. I was happy to let him, since Zen seems to think the sun shines out of his backside, but Zen is my dog and my responsibility. Zak shouldn't feel bad about getting a job, not in this day and age, when unemployment is so high and I'm—god, I'm proud of him. It takes some determination and guts.

"I'm sure Zen will c-cope," I assure him.

He smiles and nods but still doesn't seem as happy as he should be.

"W-well done, b-by the way." I pat his arm, and his smile broadens then disappears again. He still doesn't look content. In fact, he looks even more worried.

"It also means I might not be able to do the evening walk." He waves his hands about him, and the pride I feel is tainted with disappointment, which I quickly quash. Zen and I have no right to any of his time. It's been a privilege, and I knew it wouldn't last forever. "The job is at a twenty-four-hour store," he continues, "and I start late and finish later." He frowns. "I took it because it means I can still help Mom in the mornings."

He sets off round the lake again, his expression strangely conflicted. I don't understand why. It's admirable that he's looked for a solution that would suit both him and his mother. I shouldn't factor into this, but it seems I do, or at least the time he spends with Zen does. I catch him up.

"W-what t-time do you f-finish?" Maybe he doesn't have to miss out on all of his time with me…er…I mean Zen.

"Nine p.m., five days a week." He huffs. "I had to take it, Niall. I've got no money and I can't keep taking money off Mom. There isn't an endless supply. I mean, I got money, from my dad, but I'm keeping that for when I really need it, you know? I want to get a car, so I need to save up. I'm not planning on dipping into Dad's money when I can get a fixer-upper for a couple hundred pounds."

"S-so what exactly is your p-problem?" I am confused, but also pleased he seems to be back to his old talkative self. "F-five days a week still leaves t-two days free."

"Yeah, but I like this evening walk with you and Zen, Niall. It's like a wind-down before bed, you know. I love it really, but I guess you'll've walked him by the time I get in most days."

I shrug and shake my head. "If it means that much to you, w-we can walk Zen later. H-h-he doesn't care as long as he gets a walk and to play fetch with you."

Zak stops in his tracks and stares at me. "You mean that?"

"Of course." I stop too, and turn to face him. "The n-nights are getting lighter. L-later walks are n-no problem."

My god, you'd think I'd given him the earth. His eyes are so bright and his expression so full of gratitude. All I've said is that we can walk Zen later so he can still come with us. It's not as if I've put myself out or anything. Zak is acting as if it's this massive gesture. But if he enjoys it so much, why wouldn't I want to make some sort of compromise for him? I enjoy his company as well.

"Wow, thanks, Niall, that'd be great."

"N-no p-problem, Zak."

The rest of the walk Zak resumes his usual role, and once again the hind legs of that donkey are in danger. He regales me with stories of the other candidates for the job he was just offered, and how he thinks he just got the job because the others all looked like crackheads, whereas he just sounds like one. I laugh hard at this, since he does sometimes talk so fast it sounds like he's on speed or something similar. He fits more words into one breath than most people fit into an entire conversation.

Chapter 10

In which Zak finds out I am a nerd

"H EY, ARE YOU busy?" Zak walks past me—with Zen trotting at his feet—when I answer the door. He doesn't wait for me to reply.

He never disturbs me anyway, even if I am busy. He just entertains Zen and watches my TV because I have more channels than he does; plus I have the movie and sports package, which I pay for but rarely watch, so he's welcome to. He also logs on to my wi-fi, which I suppose he could conceivably do from his own house, since I'm sure my wi-fi reaches that far.

Anyway, he always asks, but I never say no.

Today, I have quite a bit of work to get through, so I leave him to channel hop while I go to my office to put my nose to the grindstone.

Zak appears at my office door about twenty minutes later, casually leaning against the frame, one hand hanging effortlessly from the top. I'd have to stand on a stool to reach that high. He's not that bulky, but he's lean and firm and wiry. I can tell from here that he works out, and I know he runs, so he's fit. He has a hint of a six-pack pushing against his T-shirt. I fight the urge to lick my lips.

"Want a coffee?" he asks, completely oblivious to the thoughts in my head. Thoughts that I quickly dismiss and bury deep.

It's all right to look, I tell myself about a hundred times a day, *but not all right to touch.*

"Y-yes please." I smile, meeting his eye briefly before looking back down at my laptop screen. I still manage to get the full force of his brilliant smile.

He disappears to make me coffee. He doesn't have to ask how I take it. He knows; he's done this dozens of times now. Not for the first time, I wonder what he's doing here. He could be anywhere. His job seems to be broadening his horizons and widening his circle of friends, which means I don't see him as often. But still, he comes whenever he's free, which is at least four times a week, plus most weekends.

We now walk Zen a little later in the evening, as promised. My dog thinks he has two homes. *He's just a mutt slut.* I laugh at my rhyme as Zak walks in with my coffee.

"And what has you so cheerful today?" He smirks at me, and I narrow my eyes.

"N-nothing."

He places my mug down on the coaster by the side of my laptop and perches himself on the edge of my desk.

"What is it that you actually do, Niall?" he asks, craning his neck to try and get a good look at my screen.

He's asked me before, but all I could stutter out was that I worked from home. He guessed it was something to do with computers. I suppose that was enough to satisfy his curiosity at the time.

"C-c-computer c-c-coding," I manage to get out this time. I wait for the inevitable yawn, but he actually looks pretty impressed.

"You are kidding me!" he exclaims, jumping down from the desk and crouching beside me so he can see the screen better. He manages to manoeuvre himself so one arm is resting on my lap. His head is tucked beneath my arm so I am almost forced to hug him as I try to type. Okay, so I said he didn't usually bother me, but this is a bit beyond a joke. I can smell his clean, just-showered scent, and it's doing crazy things to my senses. "What kind of coding do you do, Niall? Is it like for games and stuff?"

"No!" I chuckle, since this is probably the source of his excitement. "Websites mostly. S-sorry if that doesn't appeal to your g-gaming generation!"

He clicks his tongue. "You make me sound like a kid." He arches one eyebrow, and I can tell I've insulted him.

I know he isn't a kid, but he is quite a bit younger than me: a different generation, in actual fact. I don't want him to be offended, though.

"S-sorry, Zak."

"That's okay." He waves away my concern. "Besides, you act like I should be disappointed that you code for websites. You're a nerd, and nerds are pretty damn cool."

I chuckle and shake my head, sometimes he says the funniest things.

"You must be hella clever. I wouldn't know where to start with computer coding." He continues, "I did some coding at school, but nothing so complicated and intricate as website design, and I'd love to be able to create games, but I'm a bit of a dope unless I'm actually playing them, then I'm fucking awesome." He nods and smiles proudly, and I can't help laughing.

"Tsk!" I click my tongue and roll my eyes. "Younger generation!"

He gasps, then sees I'm teasing and laughs, but I can tell he isn't exactly over the moon about the fact I've just pointed out our vast age difference.

Zen decides to break the tension and barks and snuffles at Zak's feet.

With a chuckle, Zak scratches Zen's ears. "Hey, buddy, what ya doin' down there?" Zen drops a ball at Zak's feet and backs away, looking expectantly at the toy. Zak chuckles again and jumps to his feet, smiling brightly at me. "I'll leave you to it, Niall. Zen and I will play quiet, I promise."

I know he's left in order to let me concentrate on my work, but all I can concentrate on is the way he smiles at me, and the way he spends more time here than he does at home, and the fact that my dog seems to like him better than me now, and the way his presence here makes my life seem somehow more colourful when I didn't even know it was so grey before. It's certainly filled with more noise, but not in a bad way, because I could listen to his enthusiastic, cheerful chatter all day.

I hope he wasn't too offended by my gaff about our age gap.

Chapter II

In which Zak has something wrong with his face

W-WHAT'S WRONG WITH your face, Zak?" I frown as I watch him scratch away at his chin—something he's been doing constantly since he came through the door ten minutes ago.

He doesn't look up. He's using the fact that he's playing with Zen as an excuse, but he's just had his hair cut, and his ears are flushed pink. Well, that's kind of funny.

"Zak?" It's not like him to be so quiet.

I try to get a look at his face as he continues to writhe at his chin. I haven't seen him for a little while, because he's been busy with his new job. He's called a few times, which was kind of awkward; telephone conversations aren't my forte. Texting is better, and he's sent me some hilarious texts.

He told me he picked up a few extra shifts in order to save a little more money for his car. I worry that he's working too hard, but it's not really my place to say anything, is it?

His first day off for a fortnight and he's here, making a fuss of Zen—just in case the dog forgot him, he says. I doubt that would happen; Zak is not that easy to forget.

"There's nothing wrong with my face, Niall. it's just a bit itchy, that's all." He still hasn't looked up at me, but continues to scratch. I decide I'm not going to get a proper answer so I change the subject.

"W-want some dinner?" I was making enough for two anyway. Whilst I cannot understand why he spends so much time here, I have come to accept that he does, and that he'll be here whenever he has some free time, so I cook for us both.

I have no idea what his mother thinks of this, although I get the impression he is left to fend for himself most evenings, because his mum is working hard to get her new business off the ground.

I'm surprised to find I have missed him over the last fortnight, and that I'm actually happy to have him spend time here. He's good company for Zen and he talks enough for the both of us. He doesn't expect me to answer—like he reads it all in my expression, or maybe he can really read my mind. Sometimes I think I can read his. Beneath the chatty, noisy exterior, there is a deep, thoughtful young man who sometimes has profound observations to make on life.

"Niall, do you ever wish you could lick your own balls like Zen?"

"What?" I try not to snort into the sauce I'm stirring.

What was I saying about him being profound? He's looking up at me from his position on the floor where he's been playing with Zen. He has an innocent expression on his face, but I'm not fooled. He isn't a kid. He's twenty-three. He says things like that to get a reaction from me, I'm certain.

I can now see the reason he's been scratching at his face so much, however.

"What is that on your face?" I want to laugh until I see the hurt expression and the embarrassment as he tries to hide the fact he's growing a beard.

"Jeez, Niall, you'd think you'd never seen a beard before." He stands and moves out into the hall, rubbing his chin as he regards himself in the mirror that hangs on the wall out there. "Does it look okay? I never had one before, and it itches like hell. I think I should shave it off. Do you think I should shave it o—oh!" He looks down at me, startled, as I slide up beside him and study his reflection in the mirror.

"I don't know. It looks okay—a little blonde, but it'll darken as it gets thicker."

"Do you think so?" Zak turns his head from side to side, "It's only been a few days. Do you really think it'll darken? Get thicker? Because right now it looks like bumfluff. That's what mom called it anyway. She laughed at me, Niall. I'm almost twenty-four, and she made me feel fifteen again—when I first started shaving and cut my face so bad I still have a scar."

I can't help it. I hiss in sympathy, then burst out laughing.

"That is so not funny." He huffs.

"I know, I'm sorry." I take a better, closer look at his face now, taking hold of his chin and turning his head. "What made you decide to grow a beard?" I ask, narrowing my eyes in concentration as I scrutinise his handiwork.

He's frowning, but I'm not sure why. I'm suddenly aware of the fact that his breathing rhythm has changed. His lips are slightly parted, and the frown is lifting gradually, as if he wants to ask a question, but then, with a shake of his head, he thinks better of it. He answers my question instead.

"I, er, I got ID'd again on the weekend. I told you, right?"

I don't remember him telling me but I nod anyway, because I know how annoyed he gets when it happens. He's five years above the legal age for buying alcohol in this country, but he does sometimes look and, admittedly, act like a much younger man. That question he threw at me about Zen's nether regions just proved how immature he can be—I'm never sure if he's for real or he's putting on an act.

"So I decided if I grew a beard, it'd make me look older, and there're other reasons too." He looks away in embarrassment again.

Why is he so embarrassed all of a sudden, and what other reasons would he have to grow a beard, or look older, anyway?

He scratches again, and I pull his hand away from his face, running the fingers of my free hand across the light growth of hair now covering his usually smooth chin. It feels soft, not bristly as I would have expected.

"The itching will stop after about a week, week and a half," I assure him.

"Really? That long?" He groans, inadvertently leaning against my hand as he moves his head. "And how would you know, anyway?"

"I used to have a beard," I state. "I'm forty-three, remember? In forty-three years, you don't think I could have grown at least one beard?"

"Why'd you shave it off?" He's smirking, and I realise he's still holding my hand, or am I holding his? I can't remember, since my senses are suddenly bombarded: by his smirk, his hand in mine, my fingers lightly touching the developing fluff on his face.

"I-I w-w-wanted to look y-younger." I pull away and turn before I can do anything stupid like curl my fingers around his, or cup the back of his neck and pull him into a kiss. Where did all those feelings come from? I thought I had them buried deep.

"So you shaved yours off because it made you look too old, and I'm trying to grow one because I look too young." Zak chuckles lightly. "That's kind of ironic, huh? You could've donated your beard to me. I'm sure it looked a thousand times better than mine will."

"Yours will look fine," I assure him. "I think you'll suit a beard."

I think he'll suit a beard very well—a little too well. The thought is making me hot under the collar.

Zak has an unreadable expression on his face, and I'm sure he knows what I'm thinking. He succumbs to Zen's insistence that he play another game of fetch. But I'm sure, once again, he's using the dog as an excuse not to look at me.

I go back to making dinner, thankful that I was able to avoid making a complete fool of myself. What the hell was I thinking anyway? If I'm not careful I'll scare him off.

Chapter 12

In which some things can sometimes be too nice

"I TOOK ZEN FOR a walk." Zak settles down at the breakfast bench after grabbing himself a coffee and helping himself to a cookie.

There is never any formality when he just walks into my house now. I guess he feels as at home here as Zen does over at his place. Zen spends more time with him than with me some days.

"What're you doing tonight, Niall? Any plans?" This is not the usual bubbly Zak; he looks and sounds a little down.

He never asks such concise questions. He usually takes about ten minutes to tell me the events of the day, or something funny Zen has done, before he asks me about my day. I regard him with narrowed eyes as he tries to look nonchalant. He's not fooling anyone. I know why he's over here. He and his mum had a fight. A rather loud one.

I was down at the bottom of the garden, turning over the compost heap, so I didn't mean to overhear, and I tried not to listen, but my name was mentioned. Why I would feature in an argument between Zak and his mum is beyond me.

"No plans!" I inform him, "Cooking dinner. Want some?"

"Sure, what are you making?" Zak is suddenly right behind me, looking over my shoulder. He's standing close enough for me to smell his shower gel again. It's a familiar, comfortable scent.

"Sp-sp-spa...P-p-p..." I groan in frustration.

I am so comfortable with his presence I speak without thinking—and without stuttering most of the time, but it still rears its ugly head enough times to remind me it will never really go away. Zak never loses his patience, though, when I get stuck. He just waits.

Most of the time I manage to get across what I'm saying without too much problem. This time I just show him the recipe book. He lays his hands lightly on my shoulders, with a soft laugh before taking the recipe card from me. I try to ignore the tingling in my shoulders where his hands made contact.

I suspected he'd be round. I'm sure I'll hear about the argument with his mum soon enough. He knows I'll listen.

Zak makes a fuss of Zen and plays a game of fetch with him, while I get on with dinner. He's relatively quiet, but I know why this time. I just need to wait.

After ten minutes he's still not said anything, which is some sort of record, so I decide to make the opener this time.

"How's work?" He's been at his new job for a month now.

"Urgh!" He sits back on his heels and rubs his hand over his face with a groan. "It's okay, I guess." He shrugs. "It's a job. It's stacking shelves and other mundane stuff. The people I'm working with are all pretty nice, though, so that makes it a little better."

"M-made some new f-friends?" Now why does that question make my heart suddenly feel like it is made of lead?

"A few!" He grins. "There's this one guy…"

Oh, no! My heart is suddenly a ton weight in my chest. Why did it have to be a guy? Why couldn't it have been a girl? Why am I even thinking like this?

Zak goes on to tell me about this guy in detail and with a broad grin on his face the entire time. I concentrate on cooking dinner because if I listen to him I'll probably burn it all.

"Mom's mad at me again."

It takes me a second to realise Zak has veered off the subject of this 'guy' at work. I snap out of my stupor and turn to face him.

"So I g-gather," I comment, then turn back to my task.

Sometimes I talk better when I don't have to look someone, him, in the eye. He knows this by now, so me turning my back doesn't offend him in the slightest.

"Oh, you heard, huh?"

I think the entire neighbourhood heard, but I don't say this. "Sound carries further at night."

"Shit!" he cusses, heaving a deep sigh. "See, Mom thinks I should get out more. She won't accept I'm perfectly happy with the way things are. She says it isn't healthy, whatever that means. I stay fit. We take Zen for a walk every day."

I know this is one of the things Rachel isn't happy about—I heard her shout it just ten minutes ago—and I know she isn't saying Zak's activities are physically unhealthy. Wasn't he just telling me about a 'guy'? Hasn't he made some plans with his new friends from work? Did I miss something while I zoned out?

"She says I'm stealing your dog from you, or something," Zak continues, looking troubled and uncertain. "She seems to think you'd be mad about it. I told her she could just come over and ask you, but she said you would just say it was okay out of politeness. I'm not stealing Zen from you. You don't think that, do you? Most of the time we take him out together, so he's with you as well as me."

"I d-don't think that you're stealing him. I-I'm okay w-with the walking thing," I assure him, and he nods and throws his hands up in the air in apparent frustration.

"See? She could just ask you, but no. She says I shouldn't bother you. I figured you'd tell me to fuck off if you felt bothered."

"I-I w-would never tell you to f-f-f..." I sigh, roll my eyes and turn back to stirring my spaghetti sauce. "I would never say that."

Zak chuckles and steps up behind me.

"I know." He takes a deep breath and groans. "Mmm! Spaghetti Bolognese is my favourite, Niall." He grins at me as I glance at him over my shoulder, and the effort I made seems all worthwhile. "My dad used to make Bolognese for me on nights Mom was at work." He so rarely talks about his dad, I feel myself holding my breath in case it stops him from revealing more. "We'd see how many stains we could get on our shirts. Mom would go crazy, but I think it made her laugh too. She doesn't laugh so much now, I wish she…"

He stops with a gasp, and I turn in shock, since he never stops mid-sentence. He never stops between sentences either. A break means there's something wrong, and I'd be right. Oh, god. He's crying.

"Zak!" I exclaim as he turns away from me, wiping his eyes.

"I'm okay, I'm okay," he whispers, but I know he's not. I can feel that he's not.

I don't even think about it, I move to his side and wrap my arms around him, wondering if he's ever really cried since his dad died, wondering if he's ever allowed himself to. It's like he's made it a taboo subject.

I hold him as he sobs, and he melts against me, my shoulder the perfect place for him to lay his head. He fits so well there, it's like we were moulded together. As I stroke his hair and whisper soothing nothings, he weeps, and I just let him work through it. His arms find their way around me, and for a moment time stands still, and so does my breath, heart, everything because holding him feels so damn good. The heat of his body merges with mine, sending signals everywhere at once. He feels great. He smells great. I can't help turning my face into his neck and taking a deep breath…

"Sorry!" He pulls away so fast I almost overbalance. "Shit, I'm a bundle of laughs tonight, huh? I didn't come here to offload my problems." He won't meet my eye. I think he knows what was happening just now. I think he knows what I just did.

"Zak!" I shake my head, too affected by the embrace to say anything constructive. I should apologise, but that would mean admitting what I've done, and I can't even admit it to myself even though my body sure as hell knows what was going on.

Apologising would run the risk of alerting him to what I was doing, when his embarrassment could simply be due to his emotional outburst. I want to tell him I am fine with it, that he can come here anytime and talk, that I'll always be here for him. That he's made my life so much brighter since he blasted into it two months ago.

But how can I tell him without it taking me a month? And without it seeming completely inappropriate. I want to reach out to him and pull him back into my arms, where I can convey all these things with a touch, with a kiss… Oh god, where did that thought come from? That's not what he needs from me at all.

"Niall, I think maybe I should go." He looks unhappy, his eyes are red, and still bright with tears, but there's something else in his expression that I can't read. I don't want to look too closely either, in case it's something I don't want to find, like revulsion, or anger.

I think it probably is best that he goes, so I nod instead of protesting. He bites his lip, looking disappointed. Why would that be? Maybe I read the situation wrong. Maybe he hasn't noticed how I reacted to the embrace.

"I-I shouldn't've come." He sniffs. "I-I'm sorry, Niall." Now he's stuttering. What the hell?

"B-but dinner?"

God, get over yourself, Niall. He's not bothered how long you've spent cooking something you already knew was his favourite. He's upset, and he's probably freaked out by the fact that his neighbour is basically a pervert, holding him too tight, and breathing in his scent like a crazy stalker.

"Your Bolognese will probably taste better without me here to spoil it for you." He gives me a weak smile. "Thanks for listening, Niall." Then he leaves before I can stop him. God, I think he was still upset. I heard his voice hitch when he said my name.

I don't go after him. I don't dare. Anything I say will simply highlight what I did.

I guess time will tell if he's coming back.

Chapter 13

*In which there is no fallout whatsoever
and that's just more confusing, not less*

H AVE YOU HAD dinner yet?" Zak calls as he walks in with Zen, presumably at his heels since I haven't seen my traitorous dog since early this morning.

I can hear Zak helping himself to coffee.

I haven't seen him since that night when I hugged him a little too long and too closely. It's only been a few days, and now he's working it's not that unusual a gap between visits, but it was still the longest two days of my life waiting for the fallout.

"I-I h-haven't st-started anything," I call from my office.

What the heck? He just swans in like there's nothing wrong. So maybe there isn't, and maybe his leaving so abruptly two nights ago really was due to his embarrassment over having me see him cry rather than anything else.

He usually comes straight through to the office when he hears I'm in there, but he doesn't, and I can hear him clattering around in my kitchen. What the hell is he doing in there?

When I wander in, armed with an empty coffee mug so it doesn't look like I'm just in there to check on him, he seems to have an entire three-course dinner set out on the bench.

"Aw, man, I was gonna surprise you." He grins as he takes my mug from me and fills it from a freshly made pot of coffee.

"D-did you make dinner?" I am absolutely blown away. He wanted to surprise me, and he has. I'm surprised beyond belief.

"Do you think I did?" Zak flicks his eyebrows comically, and I laugh.

"Somebody did. If it wasn't you, then who?"

"Maybe it was Zen." He smirks as he turns away to rearrange something on the bench.

Zak is being very coy as he fetches more trays of food from two bags on the floor while Zen sniffs around them eagerly.

"I know it wasn't Zen, b-because Zen can't c-cook." I meet his gaze. "I t-tried t-teaching him, but he kept drooling in the sauce."

Zak laughs and his blue eyes twinkle. What is he up to? When his eyes twinkle like that, he's up to something, and it makes my heart skip a beat as I wonder what it might be.

"You're always cooking for me, Niall, and I love your cooking, don't get me wrong. But I didn't want you to think I was taking you for granted." His smile has morphed into something far more gentle. "Also, I was an ass running out on you the other night. I didn't call, either, because I was so wrapped up in myself. Stupid, huh?" He shakes his head, not waiting for an answer.

I don't think he really wants one, even though the answer would be that he is most definitely not stupid.

"Anyway," he continues, "Mom catered for a wedding at lunchtime, and she came back laden with all this food. She had to go back out to do a buffet somewhere else, so she left this all for me. There's too much for one—too much for ten, actually—but I thought we'd share. And it's my way of saying sorry for dropping all that emotional crap at your feet then running off like a total drama queen. I also wanted to say thanks for being so damn sweet about it all. You're the best, Niall!"

"Oh!" That's all I can think of to say? Jesus, how bloody lame and ungrateful do I sound? But after what he's just said I think my brain might just have gone *pop*.

His words are muffled by chunks of pulled pork while he gives his lengthy explanation, most of which sweeps over my head. All I can concentrate on is the fact he thinks I'm sweet, and that I'm the best.

God, how bloody soft am I? I might as well get myself a kitten and paint my house pink.

He's apologising to me? I was the perverted one that sniffed his hair while he was crying on my shoulder. He doesn't seem to be in any way affected by that. Was it all imagined on my part? I didn't imagine how great his hair smelled, or how amazing it felt to hold him so close, but am I worrying about nothing? He certainly doesn't seem to think I was doing anything wrong. Maybe I wasn't. Maybe I just smelled his hair because it was there, and I got a little caught up in the moment because holding him felt so fucking fantastic…

"…so how would you like it?" Zak is licking his lips as he says this, and I think I might implode. I suddenly can't breathe, and I know he didn't mean it the way I'm thinking. "I mean your dinner, Niall." He clicks his tongue, and I feel my face heat up to burning because he read my expression. Of course he did, because he can read my bloody mind.

"D-d-d-d…" I let out a frustrated breath and turn away. I was doing so well, and then it all went downhill when I let my libido take over my brain.

"Niall?" Zak sounds concerned as he steps closer to me.

God, the last thing I want is him closer to me. That'll just make it worse.

He is standing right behind me, one hand laying gently on my shoulder. His touch infuses my entire body with a warmth I haven't felt in a long time—in fact, a warmth I haven't ever felt.

"Do you want me to serve the food up?" he asks, oblivious to my turmoil. "In here, or in the living room so we can eat off our laps and watch a movie?"

I nod and move away, giving my answer by walking into the living room rather than saying it out loud and taking so long the food will get cold.

What is going on here? What exactly is our relationship? What exactly can it be? Was Zak flirting with me? If he wants things to progress beyond friendship, why doesn't he make a move? Does he think I'll reject him? This is all so confusing, and it's not as if we can actually sit down and have a proper in-depth conversation about it. It would take me a year to ask all those questions and, because of his tendency to use a hundred words where one would suffice, another year for him to answer.

"You know, Mom suggested I try cooking sometime. I mean more than just opening a can and nuking shit in the microwave." Zak flicks his eyebrows as he enters carrying two plates laden with food. "I could try, but I doubt you'd let me loose in your kitchen, right?"

I want to laugh at the assumption his first real adventures in cooking would take place in my kitchen. His mum is a professional caterer. Why can she not teach him to cook?

"I told her you like to cook. Is that okay? I mean, that I just let you get on with it? I said I help sometimes." He regards me with an eager expression.

I nod in agreement because cooking is a pleasure, doubly so when I have someone to cook for. I'm still stuck on the fact that he thinks he'd be using my kitchen to cook in. He does make me laugh sometimes, well, lots of times, actually.

"I guess I should start cooking some stuff myself." He continues, interrupting my thoughts. "But then I think I've got a good deal goin' on here, Niall. What d'ya think?"

He winks. What the hell? I can't even look at him, because he must know what that does to my insides. He must know I'm attracted to him.

"Y'know, with Mom being a caterer, and you being the best cook ever, a guy could get real lazy."

Oh, that's what he means!

The rest of the evening I don't say a word in case I stick my foot in my mouth big time. I seem to be reading Zak's meanings wrong all the time. Zak doesn't even appear to notice that I'm even less forthcoming than usual. He just talks enough for the both of us, as always.

I think I was wrong about him knowing I'm attracted to him. He doesn't seem to be acting any differently at all, except I think he may have reached his food limit. I would never have believed that if I wasn't seeing it with my own eyes.

He's currently lying across my sofa, his stockinged feet pressed against my leg, because he's so long he doesn't quite fit when we sit on the same couch. I'm trying to ignore the way his toes seem to keep massaging my thigh. I don't think he's doing it consciously. I think he just has twitchy toes.

He's holding his stomach and groaning. We've both just had the biggest helping of profiteroles I have ever attempted to eat. I didn't finish mine, but he persevered, and now he's paying the price. I can't help laughing.

"Oh my god, I don't think I'll eat again for a week." He moans. "If I move I will barf. Jeez, my Mom can cook." I nod in agreement. "I'd get her to do this every time she caters for a lunch, but I think it would kill us both."

I feel a little more relaxed now that I realise he isn't acting differently towards me after all and all my misinterpretations of his actions were just my over-active imagination.

"C-c-coffee?" I ask. It's the first word I've spoken in over an hour. Zak lifts his head and smiles in apparent delight, as if that word is the best word I have ever uttered.

"Sure, Niall. Coffee would be great."

Chapter 14

In which I get an unwanted visitor

H I, NIALL, I'M ho...holy crap, I mean I'm back. I picked up some milk because we were...I mean you were all out, and I got some other stuff for later..." Zak's voice fades away as he presumably looks for me in the kitchen. I'm not in there. Then his voice gets louder as he returns to the hall. "...and then Zen saw that Rottweiler he hates and took off after it, so I had to chase him halfway across the..." His voice fades again as he looks for me in the living room this time. I'm not in there either. "Where the hell are you, Niall?"

"In h-here," I call as Zak appears at the conservatory door and stops dead in his tracks because I'm not alone.

"Oh, you have company." He sounds both surprised and curious because basically I never have visitors apart from him.

There are a myriad of other emotions playing across his expressive face as he notices the man currently sitting like he's been poured into the easy chair opposite me. Zak looks a little wary, but there is a slight narrowing of his eyes, as if he is sizing this man up and finding him lacking. He'd be right on that account, since the man currently relaxing in what used to be his favourite easy chair is my ex, Greg.

He turned up out of the blue, and I couldn't tell him to fuck off because he was through the door and in the house before I'd got the words out. Greg never did give me enough time to speak.

Zen, who would normally stay right at Zak's heels the entire time, like the mutt slut he is, comes immediately to my side. His hackles are raised as he regards Greg with canine mistrust. He growls, and Greg gives him a disdainful look. He'd do well to be wary, though; my dog might be small, but he's fiercely protective. I place my hand on Zen's head to calm him, grateful for his protective instinct.

Zak exchanges glances with me, and in his incredibly intuitive way, I think he has taken everything in and made his conclusions as to what the situation is. His eyes narrow to dark slits and his brow knits in a hostile scowl, because he knows who my visitor is without having to ask. One day, I am going to ask if he really can read my mind. But right now, I have to at least go through the motions of introducing Zak to Greg.

Greg beats me to it, however, because his slimy ears had already pricked up when he heard Zak's voice. Before I can even stutter out Zak's name, he is on his feet and introducing himself.

"Hello, I'm Greg," he says in a smooth, oily tone that is not going to fool Zak, I'm sure.

"Greg, nice to meet ya, dude, I'm Zak." Zak shakes the offered hand, and sounds altogether too happy to meet my ex.

He does remember that this man is an arsehole, doesn't he? One look at his face tells me his tone is feigned. He is only acting polite. I can see the hostility fizzing beneath the surface. It gives me a feeling of satisfaction, like I have someone on my side. Lord knows, I never felt I did when I was with Greg, or when I broke up with him, since all my so-called friends took his side.

"So, Zak, do you live here?" Greg is fishing, in the same feigned politeness. What he really means is *Who the hell are you?* and *Are you a threat I need to eliminate?* because he always was a jealous son of a bitch.

"What?" Zak gasps, meeting my eye and smirking. "No, dude, I don't live here, I live next door."

"So you just came over to walk the dog?" Greg nods in apparent understanding, of what, I don't know. "I see." He smiles in a condescending way. "I get it now." He turns to me, deliberately turning his back on Zak, and shakes his head in disappointment. "You know, I told you not to get that dog if you weren't able to walk it, Niall." He leans towards me, ignoring Zen's low growl and Zak's soft gasp. "So why don't you pay the guy, and then we can get on with our conversation?" He says the last words in a low tone, and backs it up with a suggestive click of his tongue. Jesus, I'm not a horse.

Greg stretches out a hand to touch me but pulls it back when Zen gives another warning growl. He regards my dog with more than a little venom. There was a time when Greg's possessiveness thrilled me and made me feel wanted. It just makes my skin crawl now, because I see it for what it really is: control. His words were meant to outrage and undermine, and the tactic has worked, because Zak looks irate.

"Look, dude, I don't…" Zak splutters before I jump up and grab his arm, pulling him away. Zen follows, giving Greg a disdainful look, if that is even possible for a dog.

Zak glares at Greg as I pull him away. His blue eyes are flashing, and his lips are set in a thin, angry line. He's kind of hot when he's all angry and spitting like this. I shake my head to clear it. I'm afraid if I don't defuse the situation right now, fists are going to fly.

When we are in the kitchen and safely out of Greg's earshot, Zak's expression changes. He looks…not angry that I've dragged him away, or even angry that Greg assumed he was the paid help, or that I just let him assume that. He looks concerned.

"So that's the infamous Greg, then?" He is searching my face; I'm not sure what for. I nod, a sense of inevitability washing over me.

Greg visits me about every six months or so, just to keep me on my toes, I guess. Plus he used to live here, so I suppose even after five years he still has some sort of connection to the building, even if it isn't to me personally. So it was just a matter of time before Zak met Greg. I just wish I could have warned Zak about how controlling Greg can be. We've never really talked about it, except for me to say my ex was an arsehole and I eventually plucked up the courage to tell him to fuck off out of my life.

I have no way of defending Zak from him. Greg just says these horrible things, and he knows I can't fight back. I feel helpless and weak and stupid and also mortified that I couldn't correct Greg's assumption that I pay Zak to walk my dog.

"Niall." Zak stands right in front of me, takes me by the shoulders and looks directly into my eyes. "Tell me if I'm jumping the gun here, or if I'm out of line or crossing a line or whatever, but do you want that asshole in your house?"

"I-I-I…" I huff. Greg has rendered me without words. He always could reduce me to a gibbering wreck. He comes round here because of that. He likes to feel strong, and when he's with me he feels on top of the world, because he's basically a bully.

"You don't have to say anything, Niall. Just nod or shake your head. Did he turn up out of the blue?"

I nod, a little dumbstruck for another reason now, because Zak is an extremely perceptive young man.

"Did you invite him in?"

I shake my head. Greg didn't wait for an invite; he just barged in, like he thinks he still owns the place, not that he ever did in the first instance, but still…

"Do you want me to kick his ass out of the house?"

I shake my head vigorously. I don't want Zak to get into trouble, and Greg is the kind of person who could cause a lot of trouble.

"Do you want me to send Zen in there to bite his ass?"

I laugh out loud at his suggestion as Zen jumps and yelps at my feet at the mention of his name. I know for a fact that Zen would do exactly what Zak asked of him. Not only that, but I'm pretty certain Zak would be right behind him, ready to kick Greg out of my house. I'm tempted—very tempted—but again, I don't want Zak, or Zen for that matter, to get into trouble.

"N-no, h-he'll leave soon. H-he just came round t-to—"

"To make you feel like you're two inches tall," Zak interrupts me, and I give him a shocked look, since he never interrupts me, like really, never. Since the moment we first met, he has always allowed me to get there on my own. He has never put words in my mouth.

I think he realises what he's done, because he looks sheepish and lowers his gaze, shuffling his feet. He's acting like he's done something wrong, but he hasn't. He didn't interrupt me out of impatience; I think he's just as stressed as I am about this.

"Jeez, I'm sorry, Niall, really." He frowns in concern as he looks up at me again. "I should've let you finish. Do you guys have stuff to talk about? Do you want me to leave?"

Oh god, no! I shake my head. "St-stay. P-please?" I'm filled with panic at the thought of him leaving, and he certainly hasn't done anything to upset me, the exact opposite. Everything he does is fucking amazing. I just can't tell him that right now.

Zak sets his mouth back into a thin, disapproving line, and I know he isn't disapproving of my request, because he is looking in the direction of the conservatory. He nods, a dark, determined scowl creasing his usually open features.

"I'll stay, but if that asshole says or does anything I don't like, or even hints about saying or doing anything, or even looks like he might be thinking about it, I am gonna take him by the scruff of the neck and drop kick his ass down your porch steps, and Zen is gonna help me, aren't you, Zen?" Zen yelps, as if in agreement. I can't help laughing. Zak positions himself behind me and squeezes my shoulders. "Okay?" I realise he is massaging me, like a coach would a player before an important game. I nod, wanting to laugh at his quirky ways. He's giving me a pep talk! "You go back in there, Niall, give 'im hell, and I'll make coffee."

I shake my head, seeing the flaw in this plan. Greg already sees Zak as the hired help; if he goes off to make coffee, that will only reinforce the misconceptions. Greg needs to understand Zak's status in this house, even if it is a little difficult for me to pinpoint exactly what that is myself.

I need a break from Greg's constant grinding at my self-esteem anyway, and maybe Zak's mouthy, quick wit will cut Greg down to size. I reach back and grasp his hand in gratitude then turn to face him.

"N-no, I'll m-make c-coffee."

"Will you indeed?" Zak gasps. "And I suppose you want me to go in there and make small talk with Mister Slime Ball?"

I roll my eyes and he rolls his, and then he pulls me into a hug with a soft chuckle that vibrates through me due to the close contact. The hug leaves me reeling as he leaves the kitchen still laughing, Zen at his heels.

Well, that was unexpected. I am momentarily weak at the knees and completely dumbfounded. Zak can sometimes be quite demonstrative. I guess it's in his nature, but it leaves me breathless and confused. I don't think he would be so touchy-feely if he knew the effect it had on my body.

I make some fresh coffee, glad of the break from Greg's prying eyes for another reason completely, since I'm sure he would see straight away my feelings for Zak are more than simply friendship. He would use it against us both, making sure he undermines our friendship in any way he can. I've been a victim of his spite too many times.

I'm just getting mugs ready when the front door slams. Zen runs back into the kitchen, and I feel my heart sink. This can only mean one thing. Greg has insulted Zak enough to make him leave, or worse, he's told Zak to leave, which he has no right to do.

I glance down at Zen in alarm then run to the front door in a panic. It isn't Zak leaving, though. It's Greg. I get there just in time to see his car pull out of the drive, the tyres screeching on the tarmac in his haste to get away. He doesn't even look back.

Oh god, what has he done to Zak?

I run into the conservatory to find an apparently unscathed Zak staring out into the garden, his back to me. I can see by the set of his shoulders he isn't happy.

"What the hell?" I gasp, feeling utterly confused. "Wh-what happened?"

"Greg the Asshole left," Zak tells me in a matter-of-fact tone, although there is a slight tremor to his voice, which I realise is white-hot fury when he turns to face me. "He is a real piece of work. He told me..." He pulls at his hair and gives a loud, angry growl, turning away. "You don't even wanna know what he said. Suffice it to say, he insulted you, me and the entire gay, lesbian, transgender and bisexual cross-section of society within five seconds of opening his sorry little mouth."

Zak growls again as he recalls the encounter then throws his hands out towards the front door and Greg's exit route. "Is he for real? And as if insulting you wasn't enough, he made a move on me. When I shot him down he actually asked me how much you were paying me, because he'd double it. Jesus, he made me feel dirty. Did you really live with that guy for ten years? I think I need a shower because the thought of him even coming close to touching me is making my skin crawl. The thought of him touching you is making me feel sick to my stomach."

The thought of Greg touching Zak is making me want to vomit as well. I am suddenly struck with the urge to go after Greg and punch him in the face. He was never the most faithful of men, but for him to make a move on my... Oh god! Zak isn't my anything, what am I thinking?

"Hey, Niall, are you okay?" Zak suddenly sounds very concerned, and he's by my side before I can reply.

My ears are ringing, and my head is spinning with the strength of the feelings this situation has invoked. Zak's protectiveness is overwhelming. I had no idea.

"I-I'm f-f-fine, Zak." I shrug him off because he's put his arm around my shoulders, for fuck's sake. As if what he's said isn't enough, he has to go and back it all up with physical contact. I need to get away from him before I spontaneously combust. "I-I n-n-need to g-go t-to, t-t-t-to the b-b-b..." Urgh!

I don't wait for my mouth to catch up; I disappear along the hall to my downstairs toilet, where I lock myself in and hope he will just leave before I get any ideas. How can he be so fucking clueless about the way he acts towards me?

"Niall?" He knocks on the toilet door, and stupidly, I look about me for possible exits, like he would actually come in, and as if I could actually get away from him if he did. "You okay, man?"

"Y-Yes."

"Your coffee's getting cold, bud."

"O-okay."

"I have to go, because I promised Mom I would be home for dinner tonight, and she gets all diva on me if I don't turn up."

"O-okay." I face-palm and draw my hand down over my nose and mouth, pulling down my bottom lip as I do. Could I sound any more lame?

"I'm sorry about what happened with Greg," Zak continues, oblivious to my anguish. "He really got to me. I kind of told him to fuck off, and I wasn't too nice about it. That's why he left. So, I'm sorry if you guys had something important to discuss, and I'm truly sorry if I crossed a line, but he really did make me feel uncomfortable, and the things he said about you don't even bear repeating. He's lucky he left in one piece, Niall, and I'm sorry about that too. I should have a better handle on my temper. But when it comes to y...ah, shit." I hear him sigh and imagine him pinching his nose and screwing up those lovely eyes of his as he thinks what to say next. "Look, what I'm trying to say is please don't be too mad at me?"

Oh god, he thinks I'm hiding in here because I'm angry with him. I want so desperately to go out there and tell him I'm not angry with him at all. He made Greg leave. I have no idea how he did it, because Greg was never that easily intimidated. Whatever he did, the chances are, if Zak hadn't been here, Greg would have ended up staying the night, and I would have hated myself in the morning because he would just have been using me. The truth is, Greg only ever comes around when he wants something from me, like sex, and no matter how much I hate it, he can manipulate me like a puppet. Zak saved me.

"Okay, I'm gonna go, Niall, but if you want, you are welcome to come have dinner with us. Mom said to invite you. Her exact words were, 'Invite him, or I'll post all of your baby photos on Facebook.' So if you want to save me from embarrassment that will last me a lifetime, come over ay about seven, but if you don't come, I'll understand."

What will he understand? Will he understand that I'm mad with him and want him to suffer the worst embarrassment a parent can inflict on a child? Will he understand that after an encounter with Greg I just want to hide under my covers?

I don't want him to think I'm angry with him, and I doubt he will understand that without me actually going over there and explaining it all to him. I don't know what to do.

"What do you think, Zen?" I ask my attentive Jack Russell as I emerge from the bathroom. Zen tips his head to one side with a whiny growl. If he was human, I think he would have shrugged his shoulders. "Yeah, I don't know either." I huff.

Going over to Zak's house for dinner seems the only course of action. I need to assure Zak everything is okay, no matter how difficult it is for me to do so.

I get ready, grab a bottle of wine, and make my way over there for seven.

Standing at the door, I hear my dog barking. Zen is already here, since he has his own route into Zak's house, which he takes at every opportunity. It really is as if he has two homes now.

Zak answers the door, wearing the brightest, broadest grin I've ever seen.

"I-I'm n-not angry with you," I blurt out before he has time to even say 'hello'.

If possible his smile gets brighter, and my heart does backflips. He nods as if this was already common knowledge.

"I know," he replies in a gentle, warm tone that does very strange things to my insides. It's said without his usual flare for words.

"Oh, right!" I smile back nervously, not really sure how to proceed from here.

He doesn't pull me into a hug. He simply steps aside for me to enter. As I do, however, I feel a…something…pass between us. Is the electricity that shoots through my veins just my over-active imagination?

Chapter 15

In which Zak decides to volunteer me

O H MY GOD, Niall, so this guy at the store wouldn't serve me because he thought I was underage. He insisted on seeing my ID, but when he saw it, he thought it was a fake. My dog-eared driver's licence, a fake? You'd think a fake one would be in better condition, right?"

I chuckle, because I've seen the state of his licence. I can also see the tears of mirth in his eyes that makes the blue sparkle brighter and my breath catch in my throat.

"W-why d-didn't you use y-your p-p-p-passport?" It's hard to speak at the best of times with such a dry mouth, but add a damn stutter and it's nigh on impossible. Zak never seems to get frustrated with me, though.

"I did get my passport out, but I always carry my UK one, because it's easier, and he just laughed in my face and asked me who I thought I was, Jason Bourne?"

He sighs, and I can see why he's annoyed, even though he's laughing it all off. He has a British passport but a Californian accent and driving licence. He is a mixed bag, to be sure.

"So take a test and get a UK driving licence," I suggest.

"Maybe I will." He smiles widely. Why would that suggestion make him so happy? "And you're just the guy to help me do it."

Oh, that's why! I walked into that one, didn't I?

Chapter 16

*In which my voluntary services
come to an emergency stop*

N-NO, N-NOT THAT way, it's a roundabout. Y-you c-can only
g-g-go one w-w-way..." I groan as Zak takes a wrong turn,
and we end up going the wrong way around a roundabout for
about the tenth time tonight. He's been driving in this country for
almost four months; how has he not got the hang of roundabouts
yet? "Zak!" I gasp, and whack him on the arm. "P-pull over," I
screech.

"Hey!" He rubs his arm, frowning, as he turns the wheel to
swing the car around. He reacts angrily to a car horn, winding
the window down and shouting, "Ain't you ever made a mistake
before, asshole?" He huffs discontentedly as he manoeuvres
the car onto a side street. "I can't get the hang of these stupid
roundabouts, especially the mini ones. We don't have them at
home. We have sensible stuff, like intersections and stop signs."

"Y-yeah, well, th-this is y-your h-home n-now." I scowl out
of the window at another irate driver honking his horn. "G-get
used to them." I heave a sigh, about to offer to drive home when
he puts his foot down and pulls away with a squeal of tyres and a
squeak from me as I grip the seat in shock. "Zak!"

His face is like thunder, and his eyes have this dark shadow
across them as he drives. I don't know where he's going, but I'm

guessing anywhere that doesn't involve roundabouts. I can't even ask him what's wrong, because he looks so angry I don't know what his reaction will be. I just sit in silence and wait for him to stop. I'm a little concerned, although I know Zak would never do anything to hurt me. I'm concerned about his sudden dark mood. This is a side of him I've not seen.

Eventually, he pulls into a car park that feeds a local picnic spot not too far from where we live. We've walked Zen here a few times. Without looking at me, or offering any kind of explanation, Zak gets out, leaving the keys in the car, and walks away, towards the first track, kicking stones and looking thoroughly disenchanted with everything. He's a picture of despair.

I give it a few seconds then grab the keys and follow him. I feel terrible for shouting at him now.

I forget how long his legs are. When we walk Zen, we just stroll at the same pace, but catching him up when he's determined to out-stride me is proving a little difficult.

"Zak!" I call. "W-w-w-w…" Good god. I can't even shout after him. I try to quicken my pace but he's too far ahead. I'm never going to catch him up.

I resort to a time-old method of attracting someone's attention when they're too far to hear a shout, or when, in my case, you can't shout. I place two fingers in my mouth and whistle. I've always been good at that.

The whistle is quite loud and piercing on such a still evening. Zak stops and turns.

He doesn't start walking back but he does stay where he is.

When I eventually get there, he's slumped down onto a park bench and I'm too out of breath to speak, even if I could form any kind of question about his behaviour. I slump beside him.

I can now see he isn't angry anymore, he's upset.

He turns away to try to hide the fact he's crying, but I've already seen the tears.

"Oh, Zak." I feel terrible. Did my shouting at him upset him so much? "I'm s-sorry."

"This isn't your fault, Niall." He shakes his head, wiping his tears on his sleeve. "I'm sorry for being such a drama queen."

Wordlessly, I hand him a handkerchief, which he accepts, wiping his eyes and cheeks. He still doesn't speak, so I wait. It's a nice evening, but here in the shelter of the trees, the air has become cool. I shiver slightly. I'm wearing a sweater. Zak isn't. He's been here four months, and he still dresses for California weather. I don't think he owns more than one pair of socks. I take off my sweater and lay it across his shoulders.

"Do you think I'll ever get used to any of this, Niall?" he eventually says, pulling my sweater around him like a comforter He hangs his head, and I lean forward, my shoulder touching his.

"T-tell me what's wrong, Zak?"

He sits up again with a loud groan. "Does it get any better? Any easier? Please tell me it does, because right now it feels like I'm falling apart inside."

"About what?" I regard him with deep concern.

"Everything, Niall. Coming here, missing my friends, missing my dad, trying to do the right thing for my mom." He buries his face in his hands, and I know he's crying again. It's only the second time I've seen him like this, and again I wonder who he has had to talk to about this.

He lost his dad. He had to drop out of college to support his mum. They were forced to sell the house and move to another city away from his friends, and then he followed his mum to another country so she didn't have to make the move by herself. All those transitions haven't been without stress and trauma, and all this time Zak has supported his mum but had no one to support him.

"T-talk to me, Zak," I urge him. "I mean, y-you t-talk all the time, but you never say anything."

He looks up in shock, and I realise that came out wrong.

"About yourself—how you f-f-feel, h-how you cope with it all."

"I cope." He sniffs, wiping his face. There's a hint of a smile. "Nice recovery, by the way. What do you mean I never say anything? I never stop saying stuff. It's a wonder you've only ever told me to shut up once."

"I n-n-n..." I shake my head in denial, but he raises his eyebrows and nods.

"Movies, three weeks after I moved here. You stuffed popcorn in my mouth and told me to shut up. I was so hurt. I never forgot, Niall." He places the back of his hand on his forehead, feigning despair.

I chuckle and shake my head. I know he's kidding, but I also know he's directing the traffic. He's once again avoiding talking about how he really feels.

"Zak. Don't hide what you're feeling. You know I'll listen," I urge him, taking his chin and turning his head to face me.

I look into his eyes, and I see the spark disappear as his expression crumbles. Tears well up and fall, and he takes a shaky breath.

"I miss him so much, Niall. It's been nearly two years, and I still miss him. Will it ever stop hurting so bad?"

"Y-your dad!" I know this is who he means, and I want to tell him it gets better. It does, but only because the years dull the memories, and that's hardly a consolation. "I l-lost my dad when I was about your age."

"Really?" Zak looks up with a gasp. I nod. "That's harsh." Just like Zak to worry over someone else's suffering. I didn't feel the loss as much as he does, I suspect.

I shrug. "It was bad enough, but my dad and I, we didn't really g-get on." My dad hated my guts, for reasons I couldn't fathom until I was older and only after he'd put me through therapy after therapy, searching for a cure or an intervention and I still stuttered. I was just a source of disappointment to him.

"My dad was my best friend." Zak's voice is small, and I just want to hug him, like the other night, when he broke down in my kitchen. I feel his loss; he seems to have had a very close relationship with his dad, something I didn't have with mine.

Now I understand his fragility over the last few weeks. If it's coming up to the anniversary of his dad's death, he's bound to be feeling fractured. I throw caution to the wind and gently, tentatively slide my arm around his shoulders. He snuggles in, and like the time before, in my kitchen, he melts against me like he was made to fit there. I concentrate on what he's saying rather than how good it feels to have him in my arms.

"We did everything together, you know, my dad and me. It just got better as I got older. Weird, huh?" He rests his head on my shoulder as he continues. "You always think of yourself as getting older, but your parents always stay the same. They never age. You think they'll go on forever."

I nod. "My mum is seventy, and whilst I can see she's aged, she's still my mum. I still imagine her being able to do all of the things she did when I was a kid."

"I know, right?" Zak nods in agreement. "And I never thought my dad was old—well, he wasn't. Shit, Niall, he wasn't much older than you when he died."

"R-really?" I'm shocked now. "H-how old?"

"He was forty-four. He and Mom got together in college." He nudges me, wearing an impish grin. "She's only three years older than you, and that's not old by any stretch of the imagination."

I chuckle, but only to hide the shock. It never even crossed my mind that Rachel was only three years older than me. Bloody hell!

"Age means nothing, right?" Zak is still leaning against my shoulder, and I'm still hugging him to me. "If we let things like age get in the way, we'd die having never lived. My dad taught me that." His words are wise, but I'm not really listening.

I'm nodding and grunting replies in the right places so Zak doesn't think there's anything wrong, but the fact remains that I am getting cosy, on a park bench, with a man whose parents are only a little older than me. The thought is very sobering indeed. The fact Zak doesn't see me as old makes me feel a little better, but still.

"Thanks for helping me out with all this driving stuff, Niall." Zak still hasn't moved, and, despite my misgivings, I'm not inclined to move either.

"N-no problem," I whisper, fighting the urge to stroke his hair. That would be going too far. "I w-was w-worried I'd upset you when I shouted."

"Nah. You shouted, but you had good reason. I went the wrong way 'round a roundabout three times in a row. How stupid do you have to be, huh?"

"Y-you're not stupid, Zak. You were just distracted, that's all."

"Distracted enough to almost cause an accident. I'm sorry if I scared you when I drove off like that, but it just got to me."

"W-water under the bridge." I shrug. He takes the movement of my shoulders as a cue to lift his head.

He smiles at me, and I fight to keep my breathing even, because he's close enough to kiss, if I just leaned forward a little more...

"It's getting chilly." I stand quickly, and I hear him give a soft huff. Not sure why, unless he doesn't want to move. I suppose it was comfy, sitting the way we were.

He stands as well and shivers, handing me back my sweater. "Brrr! You're right. Jeez, it's the middle of summer. We should be in shorts and tank tops, with flip-flops."

I eye him with a snort. "In C-California maybe. This is England, Zak. We had snow in June once. I remember that day. I was a kid, we went sledging."

"Snow in June?" Zak gasps, half horrified, half excited, as we start back along the track to the car. "Oh my god. That is extreme.

I saw my first snow when I was fourteen, when Dad took me skiing at Lake Tahoe. Before that, it was just something you saw on Christmas cards."

"It's like that here, mostly. G-global warming has a lot to answer for. W-we get some snow, though."

"Cool."

We reach the car and both put a hand to the driver's door handle, smirking.

"You go ahead and drive, Niall. I don't wanna risk giving you a coronary driving home in the semi-dark." He chuckles as I nod. "Besides, your stint as driver's ed is over."

"Oh?" I look up at him in curiosity. I was kind of enjoying it, despite the stress.

"Yeah." He nods. "I got my theory test booked for next week and a practical three weeks after that. I guess all I have to do is practise, and I've got enough saved up that I can get a cheap runabout."

"Oh? From where?" I would have helped him look if he'd asked, but he sounds like he's got it all planned.

"A couple of the guys from work are taking me to the car auctions the week I take my test. They say it's the best place."

I nod, although I've never been. I'd be no good going with him, since I wouldn't have a clue. Let him go with his friends. It's certainly more appropriate than snuggling on a park bench with a man only three years younger than his mum.

"Thanks for tonight, Niall." He lifts his hand, and for a moment, I think he's going to touch my face, but instead he moves it awkwardly to my shoulder. Maybe I just imagined he was going for my face, if he's that awkward touching me at all.

"Are you okay now?" I grimace. "I mean, I know it's n-never really okay, but what I mean is…"

Zak's other hand comes up to hold my other shoulder, and he leans close.

"I'm fine, Niall. Thank you. Thanks for being a good friend. Thanks for listening, always. Thanks for everything really." Then he kisses my forehead quickly, like he's dared himself to do it, and runs around to the passenger side of the car without looking at me at all.

It's dark in the car, so I can't see if he's blushing or not. That's a blessing really, because it means he can't see my hot flush either.

Chapter 17

*In which my feelings are sent
through a blender, quite literally*

WE GET BACK from our adventure in driving lessons emotionally drained but otherwise unscathed.

Zak jumps out of the car and walks up the steps to my house. He doesn't even hesitate. I really want to ask him what he thinks is going on here, but I know I'll stumble over the words, sound like a bumbling idiot and probably rock the boat so badly he'll leave and never come back.

That would kill me.

Oh god, I feel so mixed up about this I can't think straight. Four months ago, I was perfectly happy living on my own, just me and Zen. Then in breezes Zak, and far from feeling he has invaded my life, it's like he is completing it somehow, giving me something I didn't even know I was lacking.

Zak is standing in the hall when I eventually get inside. A concerned Zen sits attentively at his feet. Zak's shoulders are slumped slightly as he waits, I guess, for me to speak, to say something.

"It's okay that I'm here, right?" he asks, and I realise he has read my expression and thinks I don't want him there, when I do. I just don't know what is going on, or whether it's a good idea. "Please don't ask me to leave, Niall. Mom isn't home, and I don't wanna sit in an empty house right now. I know I'm kinda dropping all this emotional crap on your doorstep again, but I don't have anyone else to talk to, and you listen like you really want to hear it all."

I nod and sigh as I walk passed him, patting his arm in understanding. "It's fine, Zak, stay. I-I'll m-make some tea." Did he really think I would let him be alone at a time like this? No matter my emotional turmoil, he needs a friend right now, and I'll be that friend. I'll sort out what else is going on some other time

"Thanks, Niall." He gives me a weary, wan smile.

"G-go sit in the living room. I'll bring it in."

How sad must his life be if his best source of company is a grumpy, forty-something guy with a killer stutter?

As I make the tea, I can hear Zak talking to Zen. I don't hear what they're saying, but it sounds like one of their intimate little chats, where they share earth-shattering secrets. It sounds like they're getting comfy on the sofa. Zak looked tired after all the 'emotional crap' of the evening, not that I thought any of it was crap in the slightest. I do wish I could just take away all that hurt and pain and make him happy.

I have no idea how, or when I started feeling like this. It sort of crept up on me unawares. The first I knew about it was that night in my kitchen, when I held him and it felt so good, and he smelled so good. My body has been reacting to the memory of those sensations ever since, despite constantly reminding myself that he probably left abruptly because I was holding him too intimately.

Is tonight a good time to try to talk to him about all of this? About how I'm feeling? There's no time like the present, right?

Nervously, I walk back into the living room with two mugs of tea and stop dead in my tracks. The sight before me causes me to catch my breath and dispels any thoughts or chance of a heart to heart with Zak, tonight at least.

He's lying on his back, the length of the sofa, fast asleep. Zen is lying within the fold of his arm, resting half on Zak's slim chest and half on the sofa cushions.

"Hmph!" I huff, smiling affectionately at my loyal little dog. "Traitor." Zen lifts his head and pricks up his ears but doesn't make any attempt to move from his self-appointed post.

My dog watches me curiously, as if he's trying to tell me something in his sweet little canine way.

If he's trying to tell me he thinks Zak is beautiful, then he's preaching to the converted. I realise I've always thought that.

Zak looks as if he's out for the count, and I don't have the heart to wake him just to give him a cup of tea and pour my heart out. Instead, I take the mugs back into the kitchen and return to the living room with a blanket to place over Zak so he doesn't wake up cold.

"You look after him, Zen," I tell my dog. "We'll decide what to do in the morning, eh?"

I have no idea if Zen understands that I've put him on guard duty, but he's in a better position to get closer to Zak than I am right now.

Though the thought of tucking myself into the fold of Zak's arm and lying across his chest is a very tempting one.

I have no idea where I get these crazy notions.

Chapter 18

*In which I'm working so hard
I think I may have missed something*

THE NEXT DAY, Zak is gone from the sofa when I wake up. Zen is also nowhere to be found, so I assume they are out together. No doubt I'll see them sometime today; then maybe we can talk about what is going on between us.

While I'm pottering about in my kitchen, pretending I'm not waiting for Zak to get back, I get a phone call from one of the companies I work for asking me to go in for a meeting about a massive project. Much as I hate board meetings, this job promises to pay me an obscene amount of money, so I can't really refuse. I mean, this job could set me up for the rest of the year.

I get ready and go, leaving a quick note for Zak.

***

The job turned out to be more than big; it's huge.

The next few weeks, for me, are quite literally a blur, as work takes over my life, and I barely have time to breathe let alone think about my feelings for Zak.

I am confused. I think I may be missing some important pieces of information about our relationship status—things I know we haven't discussed because I've been so damn busy. They seem to have happened anyway. I appear to have acquired a housemate by stealth—*his* stealth—since I cannot remember actually telling him he could move in.

I don't recall him ever asking if he could, yet here I am in my bathroom, and there is an extra toothbrush on the sink. 'Products' I have not purchased clutter up the edge of the bath and the bench.

When did they appear?

I left Zak sleeping on my sofa again last night, and when I woke up this morning, he was in my kitchen cooking breakfast.

"Hi, want some pancakes?" he calls cheerfully, as I wander in rubbing sleep from my eyes.

All I seem to have done over the last ten days is work, eat and sleep, and if it hadn't been for Zak, I wouldn't have done the last two of those things regularly. He's been amazing, but does he have to be so bloody cheerful in the morning?

I grunt as he hands me a coffee, and he chuckles. I'm not the most chatty person at the best of times, but mornings are particularly difficult for me, and I'm sullen and less communicative than usual. I'm just not a morning person. Zak obviously is. He's been up for ages.

I know, because he took Zen out for a walk, and then he took a shower! In my bathroom!

As I watch him prepare breakfast, I frown—or rather, scowl—at him over the rim of my coffee cup. He's not even fully dressed. He's wearing a pair of sweatpants, and that's it. Has he no shame? I enjoy his company, and I'm not complaining about the view, or the smell—he smells, *hmm*, he smells good—but we need to talk about his apparent lack of inhibition and his stealth relocation.

"Zak, when exactly did you move in?"

"What?" He laughs out loud at the apparent preposterousness of my question, but actually looking slightly cagey. He keeps his attention on the pancakes. "What the hell made you ask that, Niall? I haven't moved in."

"You s-slept here last night?"

"Er, yeah, I fell asleep on the sofa." He grimaces. "Why didn't you wake me? I would've gone home."

I hadn't had the heart. He'd been lying with Zen again, in their usual position. I covered him with the blanket and went off to bed. I suppose I could have woken him then, but he'd looked so peaceful. What I can't actually admit is that I sat watching him for a little while because he's beautiful when he's asleep. He's beautiful all the time, but when he's asleep I can watch him without him knowing. Oh dear, does that sound a bit creepy?

More creepy than him moving his stuff into my bathroom without actually asking me if it's okay? Did he think I wouldn't notice?

"Okay, if you h-haven't moved in, explain the extra t-toothbrush in my bathroom."

"I, er, eat here quite a lot?" He makes the statement into a question. I purse my lips.

"I'd noticed."

He manages to look a little sheepish, and I didn't want to make this into the Spanish Inquisition, but I find I am enjoying his minor discomfort. He does have a little bit of explaining to do.

"I like to clean my teeth straight after a meal, so I thought it would make sense to keep a toothbrush here."

This would be a perfectly reasonable explanation if it was just the toothbrush.

"And p-presumably you also like to shower and wash out the smell of food from your hair immediately after a meal, Zak, since I appear to have an awful lot of s-soap products in my bathroom that don't belong to me."

"You know I take Zen with me when I go out for a morning run, and, well, he likes to come straight home, so I thought it would be better for everyone concerned if I showered straight away. I don't have time to go home and shower before I start breakfast."

He shrugs, as if this too makes perfect sense, and in a way it sort of does. I'm certainly not complaining that he makes me breakfast when he's here…almost every morning. He even cleans the kitchen afterwards, so, you know, that's a bonus. I'd completely understand what he was saying if it was only the bathroom that had been invaded.

"I f-found two pairs of your boxers in my laundry pile yesterday." I fold my arms in front of my chest. "A-and two shirts and a p-pair of jeans."

I recall my utter surprise as I sorted through my clean laundry and found underwear that did not belong to me. It has been quite a while since I have handled someone else's undergarments. I dropped them in surprise, and I might have squeaked a little.

"I was doing laundry, Niall, and you didn't have enough to make up an entire load, so I put some of my stuff in too."

"You did my laundry?" I gape at him, not because of what he's told me, but because I just didn't think about the fact that a pile of clean, neatly folded clothes had appeared on my bed. I feel a bit bad that I didn't notice he was doing this for me.

"Yup!" He serves the eggs, pancakes and some bacon onto two plates, then brings them over to the bench, regarding me with wide, innocent eyes. "And I hung it all out on the line to dry."

When on earth did he do that? How on earth did I miss it?

"So you went home and brought over some of your dirty laundry just to make up a load in my washing machine?"

"Yeah, Niall, you know…?" He waves his hand in a circle as he swallows a mouthful of coffee and almost chokes on it in his haste to explain himself. "Thus saving water and electricity, et cetera."

I just stare at him. Does he expect me to believe this poppycock?

"So, okay." I shake my head, then nod in agreement with his logic. "W-what about the fact that you add s-stuff to the bottom of my shopping list all the time." He has actually done this since the first few weeks after we met.

"I did your shopping for you, Niall." He looks at me a little weird, and now I can understand why, because how could I not have noticed that?

"You did?" I know I lose track of time when I'm working, but that's ridiculous.

He nods. "Several times. I get store discount, so I just do it after my shift."

"You paid for it?" I splutter.

Where has my head been for the last few weeks? How could I not have noticed these things?

"You've been kinda busy with that project," Zak explains as he squeezes maple syrup all over his pancakes and bacon. "So I just kinda helped you out. Did you think you had a never-ending supply of bread and milk?" He raises his eyebrows, and I feel a little like a kid being told off by his dad. I hadn't even thought about it. "I know you bought the stuff I added the first time. That was a little cheeky of me." He grins and then bites his lip. "It was just that one time, then the next time I paid for it all."

I just can't get to grips with this. He did my laundry and shopping and cleaning, and I didn't notice? He must think I'm an ungrateful old sod.

"Do I owe you any money for the shopping?" I frown, concerned now. He has precious little to begin with, since he's been saving for a car.

"Nah!" He waves away my concern as he chews on a large mouthful of syrupy pancake. "I was eating the food too, and I've been using your electricity, gas and wi-fi. I figured the food was my contribution, and like I told you, I get store discount."

"But not that much." I turn on my stool to face him. "I can't let you keep paying for food."

"Why?" He raises his eyebrows, and I groan. I'm not getting anywhere fast, and he's managed to turn the subject around to make it look like I'm being unreasonable.

"You still deny that you've moved in?" I get back to topic.

"Yes." He doesn't even back his argument up with any more excuses, so now I'm beginning to think I'm imagining it all, but I know I'm not.

He doesn't deny cluttering up my bathroom or adding his laundry to mine, so maybe he doesn't even think he's doing anything wrong. Except, it's not just the bathroom, laundry or food shopping that is giving him away.

"So how do you explain the fact that I took delivery of a parcel for you two days ago, with my address on it?"

He grimaces, and I think I've caught him out, but he takes a deep breath, ready to begin one of his long-winded explanations. I just hold on and hope for the best.

"I didn't wanna miss the delivery, Niall. I knew I'd be over here when it came, so I put your address on it. I didn't think you'd mind, because it's not as if I'm moving in, is it?"

He blinks innocently, and I find I cannot argue with this logic. My initial goal of getting a straight answer from him is still well out of reach, because he has a reasonable explanation for everything. I can either tell him to stop doing all these things and risk hurting his feelings, or I can go with the flow.

"D-do you think you'll be staying over tonight?" I casually take a sip of my coffee and begin reading the paper he appears to have bought while he was out walking Zen.

"Erm…" His reply is hesitant, as if he isn't quite sure where this is going. "I got work, but I can come with you when you take Zen out later. Maybe we could watch a movie, if you're not too tired. If you are I'll take Zen out for a late run for you. So, yeah, maybe I might end up staying over."

"Well, for goodness' sake, don't s-sleep on the sofa. Your feet hang over the edge, and it makes the place look untidy. It c-can't be good for your posture, either. Sleep in a bed."

"Sure, Niall, but which one?" He flicks his eyebrows at me, and I feel my face heat up. I am half tempted—more than half tempted—to suggest he joins me in mine. I don't, though.

Whatever is happening here, it is moving at a slow pace, and it needs to keep moving slowly, so my brain has time to catch up. And there is the fact that he's denying everything. Maybe he really doesn't think he's moving in.

"I h-have two spare b-bedrooms. Just pick one."

"Oh…er, I thought, er…okay, thanks." He seems to be lost for words. Well, that's a first.

"N-no problem." I finish my last dregs of coffee, put my plate and mug in the dishwasher and make my escape towards the stairs. "Thanks for breakfast. I'm g-g-going for a sh-sh-sh-sh… Oh god, you get the idea."

I escape, feeling like I have got one up on him, but wondering if that's actually true, because he seems to have come out of this situation smelling strangely of roses, or is that because he used my shower gel?

Chapter 19

In which things seemed to be going really well, until...

ZEN AND I are enjoying the sunshine in my garden. It's a beautiful day, and I thought I would enjoy the peace and quiet, since Zak is at work, but it's hell. I've become so used to Zak's constant chatter that I miss it when he's not around.

What is going on with me? He's wormed his way into my life, and I didn't even put up a fight. I still don't even know what we are to each other. I've tried asking him, but he always seems to want to change the subject.

He's practically moved in—in separate rooms, admittedly—so are we just friends? Are we housemates? He buys the food; I pay the bills. I guess that's in proportion to how much we both earn.

I don't think he's actually told his mum he's moving out. I think the process has been so gradual on both sides that she may not have noticed in the same way that I didn't. Rachel works harder than any of us, and she is barely at home except to sleep and frantically bake for her catering business in the mornings. So maybe she doesn't even know her son has defected to my side of the fence.

I finished my project yesterday, and Zak's gone to the car auction place with some friends from work, to buy himself a new car—or, in his words, 'Get myself a new ride, dude'. He makes me laugh. It's like living in an American sitcom.

I'm planning on cooking his favourite spaghetti Bolognese as a thank you for everything he's done for me over the last few weeks while I was involved with that damn project.

He wanted me to go with him to the auction, but I'm no good at things like buying cars. He's far better off going with his friends. I can't wait to see what he buys, though.

It's about four in the afternoon when Zen gives a small, excited huff and disappears through his gap in the fence signalling to me that Zak is home.

"Hey, Niall," Zak calls from the other side of my garden gate. "Come see my new ride."

I can't help chuckling at the excitement in Zak's voice. I'm sure if he had a tail he'd be wagging it.

I go through the house and open the front door and then stand there gaping at Zak's new 'ride'.

"A motorbike?" I gasp as Zak straddles it, grinning from ear to ear, very proud of his acquisition.

"What d'ya think? Pretty cool, huh? It's vintage. I got it for a song at the auction."

"B-but I thought you were getting a car."

"He *was* getting a car, Niall, but he came back with that monstrosity." Rachel is standing in the doorway of their house, her hands covered in flour, looking on in disgust at her son's choice of transportation.

"It isn't a monstrosity, Mom." Zak sighs in frustration, and I get the impression they have had this conversation already. "Tell Mom it isn't a monstrosity, Niall."

I look from him over to Rachel and then back to him, unable to actually form any words because I'm not really sure where I stand with motorbikes in general. I mean, Zak looks pretty hot sitting astride this one, and I find myself imagining him in leathers and a helmet, and riding boots and…phew.

Then I see Rachel's face, and the worry in her eyes, and I remember friends who have had nasty accidents on bikes and never fully recovered. People get killed all the time, and the next heap of bones and blood in the road could be Zak.

Zak groans as he sees exactly what I'm thinking as well.

"I thought at least you would be on my side, Niall." He rolls his eyes and climbs off the bike. "Don't worry, I won't be riding it again, until I get all the gear anyway."

"You rode it home?!" Rachel almost screams and I gasp.

"You rode without any protective gear?" I can't believe he would do something so irresponsible.

Zak rolls his eyes again, as if I am acting like a worrywart parent instead of a friend. I can be a friend and still be a worrywart, though, right?

"I borrowed a helmet," he assures me. "And it wasn't far. I've ordered leathers. They'll take a few weeks to get here, so I promise I won't ride until they arrive."

I nod vigorously and meet Rachel's concerned eye. She nods in gratitude, as if I have taken her side on purpose, but I haven't. I just share her concerns. I have no wish to see Zak broken in any way.

With some discontented mumbling, Zak pushes his newly acquired bike into the garage. "The thing needs some work anyway," he mutters, not looking at me or his mother. He laughs at Zen, though, who follows him into the garage. "Hey, little buddy, are you gonna be a grease monkey too?"

Rachel comes down the steps to join me in the drive. We haven't really had that many conversations, Rachel and I. It's not for want of trying, but she's never really had time to wait for me to get my head and mouth in sync. She regards me with a worried frown.

"He won't listen to me," she tells me quietly, almost conspiratorially. Her expression is troubled. "He said he was getting a car. He went to that damn auction with some of the guys he met at work, and came home with that. I don't know where his head is at the minute."

"H-he'll b-be c-c-c-careful, I'm s-sure."

"His dad had a bike. Just before he passed, he gave Zak some lessons. He spent all that time trying to get a British driving licence and now he'll have to get a bike licence. I'm worried sick he will do something stupid. He so wants to be like his dad…" Rachel's voice hitches, and she stops herself from saying anything else.

I want to tell her it's fine to talk, but she's already looking at the now-closed garage door with a determined frown on her face. She turns back to me and brushes her dark hair from her eyes as the wind tosses it about at random.

"Will you speak to him, Niall?" she pleads. "He listens to you. I'm just his mom, you're his…friend."

I have no idea why she paused before she said that, except… if she can't work out what Zak and I are to each other then I have no chance.

***

Ten minutes later, Zak and Zen are back in my house, in my kitchen in their usual spots: Zen in his basket chewing contentedly on a treat and Zak perched on the bench watching me cook.

"So, what do you really think of the bike, Niall?" Zak asks eventually, after watching me in silence for a few minutes.

I think he's already guessed what I'm going to say, which is why he's waited this long. I just haven't really thought of a good way to say I'm not happy without it sounding like I think I have a right to approve or disapprove of what he does.

"N-not really m-my place, Zak." I don't turn to face him, pretending that the dinner I am making needs constant attention. "W-what you choose to drive, ride or w-whatever is up to you."

"But you're not happy." Zak sounds 'not happy' too.

"What g-gave you that idea?"

I check the recipe card. I don't have to, but it's better than meeting his eye and seeing irritation, or anger, or whatever he's going to feel when I admit I hate the thought of him riding that bike even with all the protective gear

With a tetchy huff, he jumps down from the bench and snatches the card from under my nose.

"Hey!" I turn and scowl at him, stretching for the card which he holds just out of reach.

"You've made this meal twenty times at least since we first met, so don't pretend you need to look at the recipe just to avoid talking to me, Niall."

He's angry, and I try to deny that I'm avoiding talking to him about this, but the words get completely stuck.

"And don't you dare stutter at me, because you talk to me all the time without stuttering now. Don't think I haven't noticed." He points his finger at me, his blue eyes flashing. He is really pissed off, but at what? Me stuttering, or me disapproving of his choice of transport?

He's right, of course. I talk to him all the time with no hint of a stutter. It's as natural talking to him now as it is talking to myself, or Zen.

Zak is like part of the wallpaper, and his presence here is just another fixture of my home. Most of the time I don't even think about it, which, of course, helps immensely. It's when I get stressed and have to think on my feet that it gets bad, and right now I want to tell him how I feel about this damn bike, but I haven't had time to think about what it is I want to say.

I give up trying to reach the recipe card with a huff and a sigh.

"D-d-don't b-be cross w-with m-m-me, Zak," I stammer, feeling my stomach flip as his expression goes from angry to gentle in an instant.

I see the regret in his eyes as he realises how his anger has affected me. I don't want him to feel bad. He reacted naturally. He shouldn't ever think he has to walk on eggshells around me. I'm not fragile, I'm just a little badly wired.

I reach out to reassure him, and suddenly I'm in his arms. I didn't expect this, and I think I might have squeaked as he pulled me into a hug. He feels warm and firm, and I can't help turning my head so my cheek presses against his chest. I'm surprised how well I fit there.

"Oh god, Niall, I'm sorry. I'm not mad at you. I know you're not happy about the bike. What can I say to make you feel better about it?"

I shrug, and he holds me at arm's length. I doubt he can say anything, but there are certain rules he has to follow in order to keep him safe.

"It t-takes t-training to ride well and safely," I offer. "Lessons are expensive."

"This isn't the first bike I've ridden, Niall. I'm not a novice. I had lessons in the States. I know what safety gear I need. I won't be riding in my shorts and T-shirt." He seems to have it all thought out.

"I-I j-just worry that you might h-have bitten off more than you can chew, Zak. Y-you got it for a song, but it needs some serious work."

He narrows his eyes. "You spoke to Mom already, didn't you?"

I grimace and nod. I think I've been rumbled. He steps away from me, making me feel just a little deprived of his closeness. He's back to being pissed again.

"Did she ask you to speak to me?"

I bite my lip and nod. There's no point in denying it, but the fact that Rachel asked me is not the only reason I am speaking to him about it. Before I can tell him this, he speaks again.

"That's really low, Niall. Of her, and of you. Did she think you'd have more of an influence on me?" He sneers, not waiting for me to answer. "Did you? What did you both cook up? Did she want you to suggest selling the bike, hoping you could get me to do it when she couldn't?"

I don't actually know if this is what Rachel hoped when she spoke to me before. She did hint at it, though, and I have to admit it crossed my mind.

"I can't believe you would take Mom's side over this, Niall."

"I w-wasn't aware there were sides t-to take." I don't want to make this into a war, but I'm not going to pretend to be ecstatic about the situation either. "And if there were sides, I'd be taking the side of reason, Zak. B-bikes are dangerous and neither of us wants to see you hurt. You can see that, can't you?" He shrugs, in a petulant, immature kind of way. "I'm just a bit shocked, really," I continue. "You said you were going to buy a car."

"I said I was getting myself a ride, Niall." Once again he sounds unhappy.

He was pissed off when he arrived, I realise, because he and his mum had already had words about his choice of transport. I don't think I'm making things better, but he asked my opinion, and I want to be honest.

"Y-yes but there's a difference between a car and a bike."

"There's no difference, Niall. A ride is a ride. And I never actually said I was looking solely at cars."

When I think back, he's right. He didn't say he was definitely getting a car. I just assumed.

I know he wants me to understand, and I do, a little, but he can't expect me to happily watch him ride off on that thing every day, each time wondering if he'll come back in one piece. His mum feels the same way.

"Th-think about it, Zak. Y-you can understand your mum's shock, when you went out to get a car and came back with that th-thing."

"Jesus!" He throws his hands up in the air and paces in a tight circle, with Zen trotting at his heels like it's some sort of game. "You sound like her, and besides, she doesn't care. Not really." He dismisses my statement with a wave of his hand. "As long as I'm not asking to borrow her car all the time she doesn't give a rat's ass."

"I b-beg to differ." Zen stops his trotting and looks up at me. "She cares enough to ask me to talk s-some sense into you."

"She asked you to do that? Is that what you think you need to do?" he squeaks.

Zen looks up at Zak now. His little head moves back and forth between us like he's watching some sort of tennis match.

"What the hell? I'm not a teenager, Niall. I wanted my own set of wheels. I wanted to be independent and not rely on Mom letting me borrow her car, or the crappy excuse for public transport you got over here. Is that so wrong?"

"Y-you could have borrowed my car. I h-hardly use it." I don't know why I didn't think of that in the first place. It wouldn't have been too difficult to get him added to my insurance. It might have been expensive, but it would have been peace of mind knowing he wasn't driving around on a two-wheeled death trap. My car sits in the garage, week in, week out.

"That wouldn't have solved anything, Niall." Zak sneers. "It still means I'm relying on someone else when I don't have to. Why would I even consider that as an option?"

"Well, y-you b-borrow m-my dog, m-my sofa, m-my spare room—" I tick off the items on my fingers "—and you h-hog my b-bathroom. You do your laundry here and you use my kitchen for your cooking experiments. You b-borrow everything else of mine, w-why not go the whole hog and use my car as well?"

Zak's scowl deepens, and his eyes seem to go flat with anger. I think I may have gone a little too far, but I am cross.

"W-what do you mean, I borrow everything else?" Well, if I hadn't pissed him off before, I have now. I don't think I've seen him quite so angry. "I don't borrow anything from you, Niall, and we talked about this before. I was here helping you out while you were working, nothing more. I. Don't. Live. Here." He points to himself as his voice goes up an octave. He's on the edge of shouting, his eyes narrowing to dangerous slits. "And if you weren't happy with any of those things, then why the hell didn't you say something?"

I give him a withering look. Why the hell didn't I say something? Is he trying to be funny?

"W-when the h-hell did you ever g-g-give me the ch-chance?"

He gasps and looks at me with a slightly hurt expression. I realise I have done him a disservice there, because he gives me all the chances in the world to get my point across.

"S-sorry!" I grimace. "I d-didn't m-mean t-to—"

"Save it, Niall." He curls his lip. "At least I know where I stand now."

"W-what is that supposed to mean?" Now I'm pissed off. Something tells me this is not going to end well.

"Well, for one, you take Mom's side over mine." Zak begins listing things off on his fingers now. It's like we're a mirror image of each other; we even argue the same. Why am I only just noticing that? "And now the truth is out." He continues without breaking his stride, oblivious to my inner ramblings. "You don't really want me here."

"Zak, th-that's not t-true. I d-do…"

"And you know what? You're right. I was kind of borrowing all your things without really asking. I know I should've asked to walk your dog, or become your friend, or even to spend time with you, or stay the night on your couch, or spare bed. I should've asked. But I was doing you a favour."

"Zak, y-you're b-being—"

"Silly? Huh? Am I being immature? Is that what you were going to say? Or maybe unreasonable. That's what Mom said. I'm being unreasonable, spending *my* money on whatever I want."

God, where the hell is this argument going? We were arguing about him staying here, now we're back to that stupid bike. We're going round in circles.

"It's n-none of m-my business how you s-spend y-your—"

"You're damn right it's none of your business," Zak hisses angrily, and Zen yelps in confusion because his two favourite people in the whole world are shouting at each other. He has no idea whose side to take. "And you know what, Niall? I'll make it even less of your business by getting out of your hair. I'll just go and get all my stuff out of the spare room, and then you don't need to worry about me invading your space anymore."

He storms out of the kitchen and disappears down the hall and up the stairs. For once, Zen doesn't follow him. He just stares after him and then looks up at me with a quizzical look on his face. I shrug.

"I don't know either?" I have no idea why Zak is so pissed off. Have I crossed a line? I think I might have offended him, but does he really think I haven't wanted him here all these months? "Zak!" I call after him and run out into the corridor to find him already on his way down the stairs with an armful of clothes and other stuff. I had no idea he had that much stuff here, yet he's still adamant he wasn't living here.

"Out of my way, Niall. I'll get these things out of your house and out of your life."

Oh god, he really is moving out, and he hasn't even admitted he was moving in. What the hell did I do wrong? He's taken everything I said the wrong way.

"Zak, what the hell? St-stop!" I shout at him as he passes me in the hall without a second glance. "Whatever I said that got you so angry, I'm sorry. I'll make a cup of tea, and we can talk."

"No!" he yells, dumping the pile of clothes on the floor and taking a step towards me in such an intimidating way that I take a step back. Zen woofs a warning. "You don't get to tell me what I can and can't do, and neither does my mother. It's my money, I'll spend it how I want, and I wanted a bike. I like that bike so the damn bike stays."

"A-and wh-what about this?" I ask, indicating the mess of stuff—not just clothes, but his possessions—strewn across the hall floor.

With a huff, Zak bends down and begins to scoop it all back up. "Don't worry, I'm taking it all. There won't be a scrap of anything belonging to me left in your house, then you can't grouch about me living here anymore, ungrateful bastard that you are."

"U-ungrateful w-wha—"

"You heard me." He cuts me off again as he stands and throws his things back down on the floor, in order to wave a finger at me. I'm beginning to get really angry with his constant interruptions. "You know how much I've done for you over the last month. You were working so hard you would've forgotten to sleep if I hadn't made you. Well, now you think that gives you the right to dictate how I spend my free time and my hard-earned money. Don't forget that while I was looking after you, I was also working full-time."

Does he think I don't appreciate what he's been doing? I've said thank you so many times it's almost an automatic reaction every time I see him. He didn't have to do any of it but he did, without hesitation.

"I n-never asked you t-to—"

"No, you didn't, did you? You just accepted it all as a given. You take me for granted, just like Mom does."

I swear if he cuts me off again I will snap!

"Zak, th-that's n-not—"

"Yes it is, Niall, and you—"

"Stop bloody interrupting me!" I shriek at him, my entire body shaking with rage.

Zen starts to bark in earnest now, because why shouldn't he join in the shouting match?

Zak's face goes white as a sheet, but I'm too angry to notice if it's with shock or fury.

"L-let me bloody finish what I'm b-bloody saying."

"Niall, I…" he splutters but I don't even want to hear his apologies.

I've heard it all before, and I've been through this all before. I won't have another person walk all over me the way Greg did, no matter how damn lovely Zak's been over the months since we met.

"D-don't you ever interrupt me like that again." I seethe at him. "I s-spent t-ten years with a man who n-never let me finish my sentences. I swore it would n-never happen again. I thought you were different, Zak, but the m-minute things get heated, it turns out you're just as bad as him."

"I am nothing like Greg." Zak gasps. "He's an asshole. Are you saying I'm an asshole?"

"Y-you're acting like one, moving your stuff out, just because I don't agree with something you did."

"You don't have any say over what I do."

"No, you're right, I d-don't, but you asked my opinion, and I gave it. If you can't cope with me having an opinion, why don't you just t-take all your crap and go?"

"Niall…"

"No, you wanted to make a point, so make it. You don't live here, and I have no say over what you do."

"Yeah?" Zak sounds upset as he bends down to pick up his stuff. "Well, you're damn right." He gathers it all into his arms. "You don't have a say, because you're nothing to me, you're just a fucking neighbour, Niall." He turns to face me as he reaches the front door and his lip curls in contempt. "You're just a neighbour with a cute dog that I took pity on because of the stutter."

With a strangled gasp I take a step back, his words cutting far more keenly than any knife would. I feel a lump the size of a football form in my throat as it begins to close up.

"O-okay," I whisper hoarsely. "Th-th-that's h-how it is, yes." I nod. I know how we stand now, exactly how.

His mum couldn't work out what we are to each other, and neither could I, but I don't even need to ask, because Zak has summed it up quite effectively with those few words. I'm just a neighbour with a dog. A neighbour he's been practically living with, but still just a neighbour.

"G-glad we g-got that cleared up really." I feel weak and sick, and I really need him to go now, because there is no way in hell I will give him the satisfaction of seeing me break down in front of him. No way! "I-I think you should l-l-leave now."

"Niall…" His stricken face is as white as a sheet, but I turn away from him, anger sizzling in my gut, replacing the butterflies I've felt since that night I gazed at his sleeping form on the sofa and thought I'd never seen anything so lovely.

Of course I'm just a neighbour. What else could I possibly be to him? I was going to tell him how I felt today. What a bloody fool I would have made of myself.

"Just go!" I snap.

I don't look at him; I can't look at him. How could he say those things to me? After all the time we've spent together, growing closer and closer every day? He moves into my life, into my house, and why? Out of pity? I don't need his bloody pity.

He used me.

"Niall…" His voice cracks, and I hear tears but I can't turn. What he said has hurt so much.

Zak takes a step, and I think it's towards me. Zen has finally had enough, and he growls. Zen might worship the ground Zak walks on, but he is still my dog and my protector. He would never allow anyone to hurt me, not even Zak.

Zen doesn't growl very often, so when he does I know he means business. Zak knows that too. With a hoarsely whispered apology, as he finally gets the message, Zak leaves with all his stuff. The door shuts with a hollow thud, and my house is suddenly empty beyond recognition.

Zen gives a soft, whine and runs to the door, sniffing it and looking up at me, tipping his head in query and confusion.

"He's gone, little one," I whisper. "And I don't know if he's ever coming back."

Chapter 20

In which Zen gets a new job

SPENDING THE NIGHT awake, staring at the ceiling, is crap at the best of times. It's worse when you know there's not a damn thing you can do about the reason you've not slept.

Jesus! This is like the break-up from hell, except there was nothing between us to break. Was there? Something certainly feels cracked.

Zak summed up our relationship in three words: 'just a neighbour'. How could he?

I know he was furious when he said it, but the truth is, even if he said it in anger, he must have still been thinking it.

I've spent all night trying to work out why his words hurt me so much, and what I might have said to bring him to that point. I know I'm not completely blameless. I did say some things that upset him. I mean, throwing him out of my house was not my finest hour. He was being an arsehole, though. He asked my opinion. If he didn't want it, then he shouldn't have asked.

What a mess. I never asked Zak to become the centre of my world, yet somehow, he has. To me he has been much more than 'just a neighbour' since the very beginning. Perhaps we should have talked about this before now; before everything blew up in our faces.

Zen has stayed curled up by my side all night, but as I get out of bed in the early hours to make myself a cup of tea and let him out into the back garden to do his business, he runs to the hole beneath the fence and disappears.

Oh crap! How is this going to work?

He doesn't come when I hiss his name, and I'm about to stomp down the garden to see if I can get him to squeeze back through the gap when I hear Zak's back door open.

I freeze as Zak's soft whisper carries across the fence through the silence of the pre-dawn mist.

"Hello, boy. Oh my god, am I glad to see you. Are you still my friend, dude? I was so worried. Come inside, little buddy, I've got a job for you."

What the fuck? Zen is my bloody dog. What does Zak think he's doing?

After four months of allowing my dog to just roam between our two houses at will, I realise it is a little late to try and put a stop to it now, but still. Zak needs to learn some bloody boundaries. He can't think I will just allow him to continue his relationship with my dog after he's been such an arse to me.

With my heart pounding in my ears, I spin around and retreat back into my house.

I can't go and retrieve Zen in my pyjamas, so I hastily dress, ready to storm across the drive to get my dog back.

I'm going to block that damn hole up!

I'm just about to open my front door when someone rings the doorbell. My heart nearly jumps out of my bloody chest.

This had better not be Zak, because he can go to hell if he thinks he can just turn up on my doorstep, with Zen tucked under his arm and a disarming grin on his face, and start over again without a proper apology.

Taking a deep breath, I pull open the door, ready to hiss at him like an angry cat.

Instead, I blow out my cheeks as my gaze lowers to find Zen sitting on the doorstep all on his own. I know he didn't ring the doorbell on his own, though. What's going on?

He isn't empty-handed, or pawed, or whatever. Or, at least, his mouth isn't empty. It's filled with a bunch of flowers. As I gape at him, he crosses the threshold as casually as if he does this everyday whilst carrying a bouquet in his mouth.

He deposits the flowers at my feet and sits, his little stump of a tail wagging happily. His luminescent brown eyes regard me with expectation. It's like he's asking *did I do good?*

I stoop down and retrieve the flowers, giving him a scratch around the ears in thanks. No one ever gave me flowers before. They're beautiful, if a little crumpled due to the method of delivery. There's a folded piece of paper tucked between the stalks. It contains one word: *Sorry.*

Oh, Zak!

How the hell am I supposed to stay angry now? He's done exactly what I wanted.

Should I go over there and accept his apology?

Maybe I should have another cup of tea and think about what it is I want to say first, because I don't have a damn clue. I never expected flowers. I never even expected an apology, to be honest. In ten years I don't think I ever got an apology out of my arse of an ex. I certainly never got flowers. We have one little fight, and Zak is sending me flowers and notes, and he's not even the only one to blame for our fight.

While I'm boiling the kettle, making tea and thinking about how on earth I want to respond, Zen disappears out onto the deck again, down the garden and under the fence.

The sun is just peeping through the trees at the bottom of the garden. The birds are going crazy, taking the dawn chorus up a notch as the sun fills them with the joy of the new day.

Dawn choruses never sound quite as beautiful when you've spent all night tossing and turning. I know there's no point in going back to bed, because Zen will need to go for a walk, I have work to do, and today promises to be a long one if Zen is going to continue ducking under the fence at every opportunity.

Ignoring the fact I was considering blocking that gap up a few minutes ago, I wonder how long it will be before Zak and I actually meet face-to-face. It's surely too early to go over right now, even though it is obvious he's awake already. How long should I wait? Will I have thought about what I want to say by then?

I'm just getting settled at my desk about three-quarters of an hour later, when the doorbell rings again.

My heart skips a beat. Is this Zak?

I open the door to find only Zen again. This time, he's carrying a gift bag. Inside are six of my favourite chocolates and another note: *So sorry.*

Zak must have taken Zen for another walk, gone to the shops on the way back and bought these. I wasn't even aware he knew what my favourites were.

Having delivered his message, Zen gives a small grunt before disappearing through the house, out the back door and underneath the fence without giving me a second glance. I suppose he's a little bit sore that he couldn't eat the message.

It's about another hour before Zen returns.

I stand in my front doorway looking down at him as he gazes up at me, wagging his tail and looking insufferably smug. He doesn't have anything with him, but behind him on the floor of the porch is the word 'sorry' spelled out in dog treats that are shaped like hearts.

Where the hell do you buy dog treats in the shape of hearts? And how the hell did Zak stop Zen from eating the lot?

I glance across at Zak's house. I still haven't seen him. He's in full stealth mode, obviously, since it must be him ringing the doorbell.

"And I suppose you get to eat this message, do you?" Zen tips his head to one side, then yelps his reply, making me jump, then laugh. "Oh, what the hell? Knock yourself out." I wave in the direction of the treats and watch Zen devour them all, leaving no physical trace of Zak's message. I do think Zen is beginning to get into his new role though.

That's three apologies Zak's sent me. Am I really going to make him wait before I go over there and talk to him?

Part of me wants to see what else he'll do.

Zen finishes his impromptu snack and gives a soft, whining growl before he disappears into next door for the fourth time today.

I'm shocked when he appears in my office about an hour later, dragging something very big, very square and very well wrapped.

How the hell? Then I remember that Zak still has my key. He must have let Zen in. He is *definitely* in stealth mode, since I never heard a thing.

I lift the box onto my desk and carefully unwrap it.

Oh my god, it's a cake. With two words iced on the top: *Forgive Me.*

The cake is still warm, and it looks delicious, but I know Rachel didn't bake it. Hers are always perfect. This one is lopsided and messy and must have been baked by Zak. He can't even bake, for goodness' sake.

This is getting out of hand. In his haste to apologise for one indiscretion, he has spontaneously baked, hand-picked my favourite chocolates, bought me flowers and fed Zen.

What will he do next? More importantly, what will I do next? I need to apologise to him for the things I said, but he knows it takes me this long to get my head around what it is I want to say, doesn't he?

I try to knuckle down to some serious work, but I can't concentrate. My heart is skipping beats all over the place. My ears are hyper-vigilant as I imagine every sound could potentially be him coming through the door with something else he's concocted as an apology.

The next is quite simply the most bizarre. As I answer the door to my dog once more, he is looking just a little disconcerted, since attached to his collar are three helium balloons. On each one is printed the words: *I was an ass. Forgive me?*

I almost lose my grip on my emotions as I unfasten the balloons from Zen's collar. I can't see the knots because of the tears in my eyes: tears of laughter. Where the hell do you get balloons with those words printed on them?

There is absolutely nothing Zak can do to top this. I have to put him out of his misery. Going over there and stuttering through an acceptance speech is out of the question, though, and I realise Zak has shown me the perfect method of communication. I could have done this after his first apology. I take a piece of paper out of my printer and scribble a quick note on it:

I'm sorry too, Zak. Come round for dinner. I hate that we argued. I think we need to talk.

Am I mad to be asking this? He's apologised, in a rather unconventional way, but the fact remains that he was still able to hurt me with a few choice words said at the wrong time. I spent ten years in a relationship with someone who could do exactly the same thing and reduce me to nothing.

There are subtle differences, though—more than subtle, actually—the biggest being that Greg never *ever* apologised for anything. Zak has spent all morning apologising for one misdemeanour, when it wasn't entirely his fault in the first place.

Enough is enough. Whatever this turns out to be, I can't let him continue to think I am angry with him.

I fasten the note to Zen's collar and send him back under the fence. Then I wait. I don't think my heart has ever missed so many beats in one day.

Will he come round straight away? Or will he wait? It's only mid-afternoon, and I invited him for dinner. Should I expect him then?

I abandon my desk, since I haven't managed to get any work done anyway. I relocate to my kitchen in order to see if I have the things I need to make Zak's favourite.

When he comes, we'll talk. We'll see what made him say what he said, and we'll see if there's any hope of salvaging what we had. Small steps is what we need to take, and—I realise—small steps is what we were taking anyway. But towards what? That is what we need to talk about.

Chapter 21

In which our problems take a back burner

ZEN SURPRISES ME by trotting back into the kitchen only minutes since I sent him to find Zak. What the…? The note I wrote is still attached to his collar.

"What's up, boy?" Zen tips his head to one side. "Go and find Zak." I point in the general direction of the garden. That's where Zen usually goes when I give him that instruction. He never usually needs to be told twice, or even once most of the time. This time, however, he stays where he is. "Go on, Zen, go and find Zak."

He still refuses to move, giving me one of his little confused, whiny growls as a reply.

The doorbell rings, and I nearly jump out of my skin. Is that why Zen hasn't gone, because he knows Zak is coming here?

I rush to open the door, but whatever greeting I might have given dies in my throat when I see Zak, and the state he is in. He's deathly pale and shaking like a leaf. Something is terribly wrong.

"Zak?"

He practically falls through the door, almost tripping over Zen who is overjoyed to see him. For perhaps the first time since we met, Zak ignores my dog and paces in my entrance hall like a thing possessed. "Zak, what's wrong?" I manage to squeak.

"Niall, oh my god, thank fuck you're here. I didn't mean to swear, but, shit, this is the worst day of my life, but it's still not as bad as the day she's having. Oh my god, what if I don't get there in time? What if it's worse than they're making out?" He grabs my shirt, desperation and panic written all over his face. "What if she dies before I get there, Niall?"

"Wait, Zak, slow d-down." I try to make sense of what he's just babbled incoherently at fifty miles an hour. I prise his hands from the front of my shirt and hold them in mine to try and ground him, because he's freaking out big time. "What if who dies before you get where?"

"My mom, Niall." His fingers tighten around mine, and I try not to notice how good it feels, and focus on what he's just said.

"W-what's h-happened to Rachel?" I can feel panic rising in my gut, but I force myself to calm down.

"Oh god." Zak swallows hard then continues. "My aunt and my mom, they were in a car accident. My uncle just called from the hospital. I need to get there, but my bike is still off the road, and I don't think I'm in a fit state to ride right now anyway. I know I was a total ass, and I know you're pissed with me, and I don't blame you if you don't accept my apologies, but I…" He stops to take a shaky breath, and I see the tears hovering, and the sheer panic in his expression. "I need a ride to the hospital, and I don't know who else to ask."

Oh my god. Does he really think I'd refuse to help him?

"I'll get my keys," I reply without any hesitation. Whatever has been going on between us, I would never refuse to help him.

He looks so relieved I worry that he's in danger of passing out. What colour is left immediately drains from his face. He's practically grey, and swaying, before I can react.

I barely manage to get him to a seat, and push his head between his knees to stop him from fainting. He's also hyperventilating, gasping for air. I kneel in front of him and rub up and down his arms to try and calm him.

"Zak, you need to calm down, okay. I'm taking you. You need to tell me which hospital though."

"Oh my god. There's more than one?" He gasps, forcing himself to breathe slower.

I've never really seen myself as a calming influence, but his colour is already returning, until he frowns, his blue eyes wide and helpless. He starts to shake again.

"I can't remember what my uncle said," he wails. "I don't know the hospitals around here. What if we can't find out which one? I don't have my uncle's number, only my aunt's, and she was in the accident too. Niall, what am I gonna do?"

He's not thinking straight at all, since his uncle just called him, so he could call him back. I put my hands on his shoulders, and he stops as I hold his gaze. His eyes are wild, like he's beyond thought right now. I think about the nearest hospitals that might have conceivably taken in car accident victims.

"Well, there are two hospitals with Accident and Emergency near here. County General and King's Memorial."

"County General! That's the one," he shouts, causing Zen to yelp. "I'm sure he said County." His hand goes down automatically to calm Zen, scratching his ears. I guess I'm not the only one with calming skills, since my dog seems to be doing a good job too.

"Good. County is only a t-twenty-minute drive from here. W-when you're sure you're not going to pass out when you stand, we'll get going." I stand and move towards the door but he stops me with a hand on my arm. He holds my gaze, and I feel myself melting inside.

"Thanks, Niall. I mean really, thanks so much for this."

I try to ignore the flutter in my chest as I see the gratitude in his deep-blue eyes.

"It's n-no problem, Zak, really." I don't add that I would do anything for him, that he only has to ask. Instead, I pull him into a hug, which he returns without hesitation, as if this is what he has needed since he first fell through my door.

His arms wrap around me, and he balls his fists into the back of my polo shirt. He clings to me as if I am his lifeline, his only hope of rescue.

I can't read too much into this. Like he said, he's only come to me because he had no other choice. After all of this is over, there'll be time to try to sort out any of the other stuff that's going on, like why his words hurt me so much, or why he's felt the need to spend all day concocting such elaborate apologies.

"Okay, are you g-good to go?" I ask him, and that's when I realise my shoulder is wet, where his tears have soaked the fabric. "Oh, Zak." He tightens his grip on me, as if I am the only thing holding him together.

"What if something happens to her, Niall? We had a fight about—stuff, after I got home last night." He pulls away and eyes me sheepishly. I wonder what the fight was about. "I spent all night worrying about that and about this." He waves his hands between us. "What I would do if something happened to you before I got the chance to say I was sorry properly, or to tell you… Urgh! Holy shit, Niall." He sobs almost uncontrollably into my shoulder, and I hold him. Is it okay to still enjoy the sensation of holding him, even though he's in such distress? "I'm sorry, I'm so sorry." Zak's voice cracks slightly. "Oh god, what if she dies? What if she can't work again? What if she ends up in a wheelchair?"

"Zak!" I pull out of the embrace, forcing myself to focus on him and not on how good it feels to hold him. I shake him gently.

He is quickly in danger of becoming hysterical, and I won't be able to drive if he's going out of his mind in the passenger seat. I grab his face with both hands.

"Look at me!" I demand, and he stops stressing with a gasping sob. "This isn't doing anyone any good, Zak. No matter how bad this is making you feel, believe me your mum is feeling it far worse. Thinking up worst-case scenarios isn't going to help either of you. Whatever her injuries, she is going to heal a hell of a lot quicker if she doesn't have to worry about you. You have to be strong for her sake, Zak. You can't freak out, okay?"

"O-okay." He nods his head, sniffing and wiping his nose with his sleeve. I hand him a handkerchief. "I-I'm sorry, it's just, it's like Dad all over again, but then I had Mom, now I don't have—"

"You have me!" I grasp his face again, my own eyes burning with tears. My throat has tightened, and I barely manage to continue. "You have me."

I am quickly losing a grip on my own emotions, which is the worst thing I can allow to happen, but he can't think that he's on his own, not ever. He has me. *He has me.*

***

It's the middle of rush hour but we still manage to reach the hospital in twenty minutes. It takes another few minutes to find a parking space whilst Zak sits biting his lip, his knees shaking with nervous energy. In the time it took for us to get here, he has been able to tell me what he knows about the accident, which isn't much. His uncle wasn't very forthcoming and just told him there'd been an accident, his mum was driving, his aunt was passenger, and Zak needed to get to the hospital as soon as he could. I have to admit it sounds bad but, like I told Zak, there is absolutely no point in going over worst-case scenarios until we find out more. So I try to stay positive.

Zak spots his uncle and one of his cousins standing to one side of the main hospital door. They're obviously waiting for him. He runs to meet them, and his uncle quickly fills him in about what is going on.

"They're both bruised and battered, Zak, and your mum has gone up to X-ray because they think she may have broken her wrist and a couple of ribs." Zak's uncle turns to me and smiles. "Hi, Niall. Thanks for bringing him." He offers me his hand to shake, which I do, surprised that he knows who I am without having to be introduced.

"Uncle John, do you think they'll let me see her?" Zak asks, helpfully telling me the man's name.

John nods. "As soon as she's back from X-ray, someone will come and find us. We'll take you up to the ward so we can wait. There's a family room."

A family room, right. Well, that's the cue for me to duck out, since I'm not family, and they probably have strict rules about this. I've fulfilled my duty as neighbour, or friend, or whatever.

Zak moves to follow his uncle into the building, but I pull him back, opening my mouth to speak, except nothing comes out because he reads me like a book, and he knows what I'm about to say.

"Don't go!" He grabs hold of my hand and grips it tight, linking our fingers together and pulling me to him. "Please?"

I shake my head, my mouth still open but nothing coming out.

"Please, Niall," he pleads again, pulling me closer, holding my hand against his chest. "I know we need to talk, and I have some proper apologising to do, but don't leave now, please. I need you."

The warmth of him infuses me. I can feel the flutter of a pulse in his wrist pressed against mine. I see the desperation in his eyes. I can't breathe because he is the air, and I missed him so much, even if it was just a day we were apart.

"I can't do this without you." He seals the deal. I was never going to refuse, anyway.

I reach up and lay my hand on his cheek. He leans against the touch, and this time I know it isn't involuntary, or accidental, or imagined on my part. This is real, whatever it is that's happening. My heart is pounding so hard I'm certain Zak can hear it. At least we're in the right place if I have a heart attack.

Zak keeps acting as if the fight yesterday was all his fault, and I can't let him go on thinking that.

"You're not the only one that needs to apologise, Zak." I stop him as he begins to form a protest. There's plenty of time for talking later. "And you know you don't even need to ask. I'll stay. I'll do anything for you."

"Oh my god, Niall." He breathes in my ear as he pulls me close, as breathless as me. "I would kiss you, but I don't think it's really the time or place. Let's go find my mom, okay?"

Chapter 22

In which I'm not quite sure how to proceed

W E GET BACK from the hospital just after midnight. Rachel is fine; she has a broken wrist and bruised ribs, and they've admitted her overnight, just for observation and pain management.

Rachel's fine. Zak is the one I'm worried about. He hasn't said a word since we got in the car to come home. Zen was all over him like a rash as soon as we entered the house, but not even that seemed to lift his spirits. He's standing in the hall, looking the picture of dejection and awkwardness. I know we need to talk, but right now, I think he needs to get some sleep.

I lay my hand on his shoulder, and he immediately turns and melts into my arms, his cheeks wet with tears.

"How do I fix this, Niall?" He sobs into my shoulder as he clings to me, his hands grasping the back of my shirt as if he's afraid I'll pull away.

I thought he'd been keeping it together too well. In fact, I knew he had. He'd been all calm and collected in the hospital after his tearful plea on my porch. He'd joked with his mum and his family. I had seen behind the mask, though, and I knew he'd only been waiting until he was alone to let it all out.

I pull him close, stroking his hair, holding him as tightly as I can to provide an anchor. As long as he needs me, I'm here for him. I have no idea what will happen after this is all over, but for now I'm all his.

"You know, your mum is going to be fine, Zak. You don't have to do anything to fix it. She'll be home in a couple of days, and then she'll just need time to heal."

"I don't mean my mom, Niall." He pulls away slightly, and I tip my head back so I can see his face. I frown.

"What do you mean then? W-what do you think needs fixing?"

He grasps my shoulders and holds me at arm's length, his gaze intense.

"Us, Niall. I mean, how do I fix us?" He waves his hand between us.

"Oh!" I really have no other answer, since I was sure he wouldn't want to talk now. It's late, and we're tired.

"I shouldn't have said what I said, Niall. I know I hurt you, but the words were out of my mouth before I could stop them." He gulps on a sob and wipes a tear as he lets go of my arms and steps away. "I wanted to apologise straight away, but you were so angry. I didn't think you would listen. I thought if I left it a couple of days, things would be easier, but then Zen appeared on our deck like a godsend, so I employed him as a messenger. I'm sorry if it was all a bit cheesy, but I just wanted to make it all better."

"M-make what all b-better, Zak?" I think I need to hear it all from him, because I know what I think he means, but we've never once discussed what we are to each other.

"This. Us. Tell me how to fix it, Niall. Last night was like a living hell knowing I'd hurt you so badly. I didn't even know how much I needed you both until I thought we might never be—oh god, Niall, I'm sorry, I'm so sorry." He catches his breath. "Please tell me I haven't messed it all up beyond repair. Tell me what I need to do, Niall. I'll do anything—anything you want."

"It shouldn't be about w-what I w-want, Zak, it should be what we b-both want. And you weren't the only one to blame. It takes two to fight."

"Okay." Zak nods, wiping tears and sniffing before I hand him a handkerchief and urge him to sit before he falls down, because we're both exhausted, emotionally as well as physically.

"T-tell me what you want to fix about us, Zak," I encourage him. I need to know exactly how he feels, exactly what he thinks we are to each other.

"I want things to go back to the way they were before I messed it all up, Niall. Do you think if I apologised, we could get back to that place?"

"Y-you already apologised." I smile as I remember the flowers, chocolates, cake and balloons. "Zen particularly l-liked the d-dog treats."

Zak nods, smiling as he wipes his eyes. "And the cake?"

"I d-didn't let him eat the c-cake." I shake my head and Zak laughs. Oh, what a lovely sound that is.

"I didn't bake it for him. I baked it for you."

"Was that your first attempt at baking anything?" He nods, confirming what I'd thought.

I'm a little overwhelmed, to be honest, that he would go to such lengths to let me know how sorry he was.

"You hated it, didn't you?" He mistakes my hesitation, shaking his head in despair. "I knew." He hangs his head, heaving a shuddery sigh. "I knew I'd fucked it up too bad, I knew," he whispers hoarsely. "We'll never get back to the way we were, will we?" I place my hand on his arm and he looks up, hope in his lovely blue eyes.

"N-not the way we were, Zak. Better."

"Better?" He shoots me a quizzical frown, and I nod.

"Better, because we'd be honest with each other, instead of edging around this 'thing' that's going on between us. Better, because you would talk to me before just deciding on a programme of stealth relocation. Better, because you would tell me the real reason I suddenly have a spare toothbrush in my bathroom, extra underwear in my laundry, and a warm body sleeping in my bed, er, spare bed—"

"I love you!" he blurts out before I can go any further, and the words stop me in my tracks. My heart's doing backflips as I register the absolute honesty in his expression.

I nod, unable to make any sort of reply because of the giant-sized lump that's formed in my throat. I knew. I realise the clues were there all along, but to hear it from his lips is amazing. Can I allow myself the luxury of loving him back? Before last night, I didn't realise just what having him in my life meant to me. And now? Now I know. I can't spend another minute without him; not another minute.

"Say something, Niall." Zak looks genuinely stricken that I haven't replied, even though he knows I just can't rush this.

He once called me an Ent, because I take so long to say anything important, and the next words I say are probably going to be the most important words I'll ever say to anyone. They will be words I have never spoken to another living being.

"Niall, speak to me," Zak urges, concern edging his tone now—for me, not for him. "You just went white as a sheet."

I think I might need to put my head between my knees. Am I having a panic attack? My heart is about to beat out of my chest. Surely he can hear it, because I can hear nothing else.

"Niall?" Zak urges me once again, and I snap out of my anxiety and scowl.

"I'm th-thinking about it, Zak. Th-these things c-can't be bloody rushed."

"I know that. What did you think I was doing moving in by stealth?" He chuckles; the tension seems to have gone from his body. It's taken over mine instead.

"Y-you could've just asked me."

"If I could move in?" He gapes incredulously, and it's my turn to chuckle.

"Yes, Zak. Did you, even for one minute, think I would say no?"

"I-I didn't know. I was never sure how you felt. You just seemed happy to have me talk nonstop, but you never gave anything away, not even when I made it so easy for you and so obvious even a blind man would've seen how I felt. Mom saw it straight away."

"Your mum knows how you feel?" I was beginning to relax, but suddenly the panic begins to rise again.

Bloody hell, what was going through her head every time I had dinner over there and Zak left with me instead of staying with her? Surely not 'that'! I mean, it wasn't even going through my head. Well, not much anyway.

Zak cups my face in his hands and looks meaningfully into my eyes. I could drown in those eyes so easily, and his touch sends electricity coursing through my body. My brain might still be processing everything, but my body is done thinking.

"Mom knows how we both feel, Niall." Zak's voice is soft as his thumbs caress my cheeks, then rub gently over my bottom lip.

Rachel knew how we felt about each other before we even did? I guess she is a mother, and mothers know these things.

"Mom was annoyed with me last night, for being such an ass, but she also blamed herself, because she thought our argument was her fault. She says she should never have asked you to speak to me about that damn bike."

"Whether she'd asked or not, I would have still felt the same about it." I lean into his caress, my eyes half closed as I wrap my hand around his.

Holding his hand feels amazing; having him here again feels amazing. Hearing his voice and his laugh is amazing. Hearing him say he loves me, feels amazing. I need to stop beating around the bush and tell him how I feel. I can't leave it any longer.

"I've thought about it." I want to laugh at the expression on his face right now. It's like barely contained excitement and dread all mixed into one, as if he's about to ride the world's scariest roller coaster. "I love you too." I nod, and he lets out this long, heavy sigh of relief before his head collapses against my shoulder.

"Oh, thank god for that, Niall. I thought you were going to tell me to fuck off."

"I would never…" I gasp, but he stops me with fingers placed gently over my mouth.

He smiles, and suddenly everything is fixed. Just like that.

"Now, tell me what you want." The meaning in Zak's tone just about threatens to undo me. There is absolutely no way I can misinterpret the heat in his eyes.

"Oh, well, I w-was going to m-make tea, but I think that can wait."

"Uh-huh!" Zak flicks his eyebrows and sticks his tongue firmly against his top teeth. His grin is wicked and lascivious and altogether far too hot.

I shake my head. "I am twenty years older than you." I feel the need to remind him, in case he's forgotten, because we're about to cross that final line that will turn our friendship into something far more intimate, and people will notice these details, instead of seeing what we mean to each other.

"So?" Zak frowns, as if this was never a consideration for him, and I realise it never was. He never saw an age gap; he just saw me. Only me.

"It might bother some people." I shrug, because let's be realistic here, it is bound to bother someone, somewhere down the line. He must know that.

"Does it bother you?" The confidence in Zak's expression wavers a little, and I immediately dispel his anxiety.

"N-no, not at all." And I can say that with conviction, because it really doesn't.

"Then what the rest of the world thinks doesn't matter, does it?" His smile is so soft and tender my heart beats out a zumba rhythm in my chest.

I wonder how I've been so oblivious to these feelings. They were there all the time. I just didn't see.

"N-no!" I agree with him. "It doesn't matter in the slightest."

"So tell me what you want." He leans close, demanding an answer.

His gaze is intense. It takes my breath away. *He* takes my breath away.

"W-what I want r-right n-now?" I'm stalling, because I know exactly what I want, but is it what he wants?

"Yes, Niall, right now. Tell me what you want."

"W-well, some make-up sex would be nice." I bite my lip as I feel myself blush.

Zak snorts. "Nothing like getting straight to the point, Niall. Make-up sex? We haven't even kissed yet."

I tip my head to one side. "Y-you know, when you get to my age, you can't beat about the bush, Zak."

"Your age! Niall, you make it sound like you're ancient, which you're not." He snorts again. "Afraid you won't be able to keep up with me?"

"H-hey!" I poke him in the ribs, and he giggles. "W-with my experience, you should be worried about being able to keep up with me."

Zak's eyes narrow, as if I've set him a challenge. He leans towards me, grabbing my shoulders and leaning in closer than he's ever been. "Just take me to bed, Niall Johnston, we'll just see who comes first."

"Holy shit!" I gasp, and he sniggers.

I stop him mid-laugh when I turn my head and capture his lips with mine.

With a moan and without hesitation, he opens to me, melting against me and moulding to me as he was always meant to. He tastes and feels and smells wonderful; like Zak.

The kiss quickly becomes heated. There is nothing like beating around the bush, and this is nothing like beating around the bush. I think that challenge might be a close call. I'm so hard I'm afraid I might pass out. I never got so hard so fast.

"Mmm, Zak," I murmur as his warm tongue licks up the side of my face.

"Mmm, Niall," he repeats, just as affected as me, until we both realise together, that neither of us is doing any licking.

"Eww, Zen!" I pull away, wiping my face where Zen has joined us in a mutual licking session.

"Zen, that's just gross." Zak huffs, wiping dog spit from his cheek. Zen must have thought all his Sundays had come at once being able to lick us both at the same time. "Much as I lurve you—" Zak scratches at Zen's ears affectionately "—there are just some things you can't join in, buddy, and make-up sex is one of those things, I'm afraid."

I take advantage of the break in the proceedings and stand, offering my hand to Zak, which he takes, a look of utter wonder and complete and undying affection in his eyes.

"B-bed?" I raise my eyebrows in query. He nods and bites his lip.

"Which one?"

I remember him asking this not so long ago when I said he could stay, rather than argue about his underhanded way of moving into my home.

Was he waiting for me to make this suggestion even then? How could I have missed that? Although, admittedly, I was kind of oblivious to all of his hints. It's only now, looking back, that I realise just how many hints he dropped.

As he stands, I push myself against him, grabbing handfuls of his shirt to pull him to me. He complies with a huff of delight and surprise, brushing the backs of his fingers across my forehead and cheek.

"How l-long would you have waited for me t-to catch on?" I ask. He grins and shrugs.

"I don't know. Forever maybe? I wasn't in any hurry, and I knew from the very beginning you always get there in the end."

"Well, you know me. I l-like to take my t-time." I know, from the way his pupils just shot to the size of golf balls, that he gets my double meaning.

"Oh, I hope so, Niall." He chuckles. "I certainly hope so."

We're wasting time, though.

I pull him down into a kiss, and I suddenly know what it's like to kiss sunshine, as he continues to smile throughout. Somehow I doubt that smile will fade, and it's amazing that it's there for me, and because of me.

Without another word, I take his hand and lead him to my room. I think there are going to be some in-depth discussions of what's about to happen, but right now, actions speak louder than words. We don't need to say a word. Not a word.

The End (or rather The Beginning!)

Epilogue

*In which I am kind of persuaded
to get a big ass Christmas Tree*

N IALL, WHEN ARE we going tree shopping?"
"T-tree what?" I ask as I regard Zak over the top of my coffee cup.

We've been officially living together for three months now. I say officially living together, because, it's actually been longer than that, but we were both, apparently, in denial about it. How that looked from the outside must have been quite ridiculous. I mean, how do you not know that you are actually living with someone?

Zak moved in by stealth, gradually, over a period of a few months, from his mother's house, so I can't pinpoint the exact date we actually started living together under the same roof. I still haven't plucked up the courage to ask Rachel what the hell she thought was going on. Over that period of covert relocation, neither Zak nor I were willing to admit it fully. He denied it every time I asked him and I kind of just went along with that because I didn't want to rock the boat. He says Rachel knew how we both felt about each other before we did.

We weren't sleeping together at the time. I suppose it would have been easier to define our relationship if we had. That would have been a step too far at the time. Zak is twenty years younger than me. No matter how attracted I was to him I just was never sure how far I could push it, so I didn't. I contented myself with his presence, which was almost constant, and the fact that my dog, Zen, adopted him from the first day he moved next door. Zak, however, had other ideas. Apparently, he was just waiting for me to catch up, but oh boy, when I eventually did…

Zen barks now and shocks me out of my reminiscing. I look up and see Zak's deep blue eyes sparkling with amusement as they watch me.

"Did you hear a word I've just said?" he asks with a smirk.

He's not annoyed or irritated. He finds my day dreaming cute. He told me once, that was one of the things he fell in love with first, the fact that I think a lot. He says, although I don't know how true this is, that he can almost hear me thinking. I always did suspect he could read my thoughts. I do often take a long time before I answer questions, not because I want to say the right things but because it takes so much effort to say it at all.

I stutter rarely now, but sometimes it can still rear its ugly head, usually when I'm upset, or angry or trying too hard to say the right thing. Zak is one of only a few people in my life that waits for me to get my head in gear. How did I not know from the beginning that he was made for me?

"I was thinking about what you just asked." I grunt, taking another sip of my coffee. I'm not a morning person at the best of times. I was up late working on a project, so I'm feeling delicate and gritty-eyed this morning. "Y-you want to go shopping for Christmas Trees?"

His question has thrown me a little. I've never been one for too many Christmas decorations. Whilst Christmas, for most people, usually means family and friends and parties and stuff, it never has for me, not for a long time. I have a small fibre-optic tree I put up in the conservatory and some garland lights I string over the fireplace in the living room but that's about it.

Before Zak burst onto the scene, I was alone for five years, except for Zen, of course. In the years before that, when I was with Greg, we always had a big fake tree to impress the clients he would invite to our, I mean, *his* annual Christmas party. He never wanted a real tree. He said it made too much mess. I never really argued. I just went along with whatever he wanted because it was easier than trying to tell him what I wanted. I never wanted the parties either, but again, he never cared what I wanted anyway, so it wouldn't have done any good trying to tell him that.

"Niall!" Zak chides. I'm lost in thought again. "What the hell are you thinking about that's making you frown so deeply?" he presses an index finger into the crease between my eyebrows. "What the hell is there to think about? It's tree shopping. It's not a question of if we're going but when."

"I wouldn't know where to start shopping for a tree, Zak," I eventually manage to admit. "I've never had a real tree, before."

Zak looks shocked. Devastated, in fact. I don't think he can quite fathom how I've ever celebrated Christmas before now without a real, live tree.

"What, never?" He gasps. "Like, even when you were a kid?"

"D-definitely not when I was a kid." I'm resigned to the fact that my childhood Christmases were not like that of others. "My parents always took me somewhere exotic for Christmas, so we never had any decorations at home. Christmas days were always spent in a hotel somewhere far flung." There'd usually been trees in the hotels we stayed at, but they'd never been our trees.

"And what about now?" Zak still seems to be reeling from the fact that I didn't spend any of my Christmases at home. "Does your mom come over? Do you go to her?"

Zak has yet to meet my mother. I haven't been putting it off or anything. My mother and I are just not that close. She knows Zak and I are living together, but I figured I'd spare Zak and Rachel the pain of having to listen to what my mother thinks is just another disappointing life choice.

"*He's how old?*" she'd spluttered when I'd told her the news. It was just after Zak and I had declared our feelings for each other and I was still on cloud nine. "*If you'd married and had children when I told you to then by now I could have had grandchildren that age, Niall, really.*"

I'd decided to end the conversation there and then. I hadn't wanted to hear any more, and I definitely did not want her saying those things in front of Zak or Rachel. My mother would not hold back, I was sure. She wouldn't care that she might be hurting anyone's feelings. I haven't spoken to her since, which isn't a hardship, because we rarely spoke anyway. I doubt she's noticed.

"My mother still goes away for Christmas," I inform him. "She decided she wanted to keep up the tradition after I moved out to live with Greg. She never saw any reason to stay in this country when she could be somewhere warm, being waited on hand and foot."

"Sh-she never stayed, even when you and Greg split up?" Trust Zak to draw straight to that conclusion from what I've told him.

It's true though. Even that first Christmas without Greg, my mother had taken herself off to Trinidad for the entire months of December and January and left me to spend Christmas and New Year alone. I don't have any other family. Most of the people I'd called friends had actually been Greg's friends, and my chosen career is conducted in relative isolation, so I have no work colleagues either. I've been on my own every Christmas ever since. Except for Zen, obviously.

"What did you do?" Zak's voice is a whisper and I see he's upset now. "You split up with Greg five years ago. Did you spend every Christmas alone?"

I nod. He definitely reads my thoughts.

"The first two years I was completely on my own. After that, I got Zen. It wasn't so bad, though," I explain. "I was always so busy working right up until Christmas, that spending the holiday alone was actually quite relaxing. I might even go as far as to say that I enjoyed it."

I know he finds it difficult to understand how I could have been happy living on my own without much contact with others. He's so gregarious and I'm just not. How can I make him see I wasn't unhappy? Because I think he's actually quite worried, which is sweet, and I love him for it, but unnecessary.

"I would listen to how others stressed about getting everything organised and how many they were cooking for on Christmas Day and think myself lucky I had only myself to please. I usually do what the hell I want on Christmas Day. I still have a special lunch, because I like cooking, but I spend the entire day in my pyjamas and never even switch on the TV. I even walk Zen in my PJs because there's never many people around."

I don't suppose Zak will let me do that this year. I'm not all that sure how I feel about it. I've already spent Thanksgiving with him and his mum, because they're from America, and that is a big holiday over there. Don't get me wrong, I love being with him. He fills my world with light and noise and laughter, but I do need to recharge my batteries every now and then.

Zak acted like a kid at Thanksgiving. He was so excited to share the holiday with me. It was fun. Rachel and I cooked dinner together. She keeps trying to recruit me for her catering business because apparently I have a magic touch when it comes to seasoning things. I always find it quite funny that she, a professional caterer, would think my unprofessional tinkering with seasonings and flavours would be any good. It was never appreciated by anyone else I know.

Whenever Greg organised a dinner party he paid caterers. He never thought my cooking was good enough. I am so well rid of him.

"I swear to god, Niall, if you don't answer me right now, I am going to go and buy the biggest ass Christmas tree you've ever seen and cut a hole in the ceiling to fit it in the house."

"I believe you would as well." I snort. I now have a mental image of Zak dragging the biggest Christmas tree ever up my—our drive.

Without warning Zak jumps around the breakfast bench and into my lap before I can put up any sort of defence. Not that I need to defend myself from him. Far from it, but he is six foot three and I am five foot nine. Him sitting in my lap is a bit like Buddy the Elf sitting in his elf dad's lap, without the dad tag, obviously, because…well let's just get that out of my head right now, because…hmmm!

"Oh-ho, Niall." Zak laughs as his arms snake around my shoulders and he wiggles around so that he's actually straddling my lap. "Someone's getting excited about shopping for Christmas trees." He nuzzles my neck and I giggle and squirm.

Until I met Zak I do not recall ever having giggled, or squirmed, but he just has to push his warm nose against my neck, and breathe hot sighs across my skin and I'm giggling and squirming and gasping.

After that, everything is a blur. It always is. Even after three months, sex with Zak is exhilarating, energetic and never the same twice in a row.

"I don't think we've done it in the kitchen yet," Zak murmurs into my ear, and that's it. I'm lost. It doesn't matter that I'm knackered after working long hours over the last two weeks, to finish a project before Christmas. It doesn't matter that I'm not a morning person—at all. All that matters is just how much his touch can turn me on. It doesn't even have to be his touch. Just hearing his voice has me in a hot mess, so him on my lap, with his hand dangerously close to fondling my nether regions, has me completely dazed.

"Zak!" I give a strangled gasp as his hand easily finds its target inside my pyjama pants. "I've only j-just got out of b-bed."

"And I am so glad, because I need you right now." His low tone sends shivers up and down my spine. "You were too tired last night."

He's right. I was asleep before my head hit the pillow, something that's happened a lot over the last two weeks. I do feel a little guilty about it. He never complains, he just saves it all up for later.

"Oh god." I almost squeak, because his hand just squeezed around my cock.

"I want you, Niall," he whispers before covering my mouth with his in a passionate, mind-blowing kiss. "I love you." He draws back to meet my gaze and I catch my breath.

That blows my damn mind. I doubt I will ever get used to hearing him say those things. How is it possible that I've become the object of such affection and desire? I'm not that sexy, except when he looks at me that way, it's like he doesn't see anything else. I'm his only focus, his only thought.

I can't speak now. My brain won't let me. I can't return the verbal sentiments, because the words get stuck. This is another of those times my stutter rears its head. Zak's name is the only word I can murmur, gasp or whine, as he climbs off my lap and lifts me onto the kitchen bench.

"I wanna fuck you right here, Niall," he growls in my ear. "If you don't want that, just shake your head."

All I can do is give a helpless moan and nod, because why the hell wouldn't I want him to take me over the kitchen bench?

"Unless, of course, you wanna fuck me." Zak's low tones continue to send signals down my spine to my groin.

Oh god, this is another aspect of sex I never thought I'd experience. Zak loves to switch. I'd never topped until I met him. He was my first. I've discovered I love it, but I think he loves it more. He screamed my name. That was a first too.

Right now, though, I need him inside me. It just feels so damn good.

I answer by shoving my tongue into his mouth, wrapping my legs around his hips, pulling him as close as I can.

"Me on top?" Zak checks. I nod. "Here?" I nod again then think of at least one drawback. We decided to go without condoms a few weeks back, but there is still the matter of lube.

"L-l-l-l-l…" I grimace. There's nothing worse than a stutter to turn off the heat.

"Jesus, you're so hot." Zak groans in my ear, completely undeterred—in fact, fired up more by the fact I can't get my words out. It makes me laugh, and he laughs with me. "Are you saying lube?"

I nod. This is the one and only time Zak thinks it is acceptable to put words into my mouth. This is the one time I'm very glad he seems to be able to read my mind.

"I got it covered," Zak tells me with confidence. "We're in a kitchen, Niall. There's plenty of oil."

He points out the array of cooking oils that are somehow close at hand. It's almost as if he planned this and made sure we were positioned within easy reach.

I gasp, raising my eyebrows in a question as I meet his sparkling gaze. He bites his lip and shrugs.

"What can I say?" He smiles a little sheepishly. "I missed you over the last few days. I was almost to the point of bursting into your office and clearing your desk, I got so horny. Then, last night, while you were sleeping, I had plenty of time to plan the perfect…nnnngh!"

He doesn't finish because I kiss him again. I pull him to me and stop his words with my tongue. Sometimes it's the only way to stop him talking. I swear he takes one breath in the morning and another at night before he goes to sleep. He's like one of those free divers who can hold a lungful of air for fifteen minutes, except he makes a lungful of air last all day. Boy does he talk. I love it. I love this. I love him.

I try to convey all that love in my kiss. I can say it out loud later, when things aren't so heated. Zak knows this, and he never expects me to say anything during sex.

"Niall." Zak pulls from the kiss a little breathless and flushed. He fumbles with the cord of my pyjama bottoms. I'm not wearing anything else. That, I realise, is probably what has him so horny, although, I never knew my body was that amazing to look at. I'm a little skinny. He happens to love skinny.

He, on the other hand, is bloody ripped. Jesus. That first time we made love, when he took off his shirt, I almost fainted. I think I might have licked him all over. I could do that now, but I'm pretty sure we aren't going to get through much foreplay this time around. He's so bloody hard.

Pyjama pants are discarded and oil is drizzled with style, over his fingers. Oh god, I hope he hasn't picked up the garlic oil, or worse, the chilli oil. He's not the best cook in the world and I remember attempting to explain the difference to him just a few days ago when I caught him trying to cook pancakes in the extra hot chilli oil.

"Ch-ch-ch…" I moan as a finger presses against my entrance. Zak leans in, between my legs, his breath hot on my ear.

"It's okay, I got the extra virgin." He snorts. Sometimes his sense of humour can be very puerile. I snort too then gasp as his well-oiled fingers press inside me.

"Zak." His name is stretched out as a sigh and I don't know why, but when I say it like that it seems to turn him on even more.

More oil is drizzled over Zak's cock and I help, because I love to see the look of pure pleasure on Zak's face when I touch him.

I pull him closer, wrapping my legs around his waist as he tips me back, holding me with his strong arms. Slowly he pushes in. Slow because it feels better that way and also because we know from experience it's over too fast if he doesn't take his time. For both of us.

"God, Niall, this feels so good. This, with you. I want this forever."

He picks his moments to declare his undying affection. Granted, this is a time to say something so incredibly passionate that it blows my socks off, but I can't reply. Not verbally, anyway. My mouth just won't form the words. Sometimes I hate having a stutter because I want to tell him I feel the same. I will, but at a time when I'm not in such emotional turmoil.

Right now, all I can do is hold him tighter, kiss him longer, breathe his name like a sigh.

"Niall," he cries out, his rhythm faltering as he draws close to climax.

I'm close too. I contract around him, hooking my ankles behind his back.

God, oh god. He grabs my cock, holding me up with just one hand. His strength is such a turn-on. His fingers are warm, gentle. It only takes two strokes and I'm coming.

"Zak, shit." I arch my back. He buries his face in my neck, snapping his hips three more times before shuddering, his cry muffled in my shoulder.

"I love you, Niall," he whispers, covering my face with breathless kisses as he pulls out gently. "I love you so much."

"I l-l-love you too, d-d-darling."

Zak gasps, wrapping his arms around me and picking me up to swing me around. I laugh helplessly, knowing it's useless to try and get him to stop.

"This Christmas is gonna be the best one ever, Niall, I promise you." He finally lowers me back onto the bench and hands me my pyjama pants.

We're a bit of a mess, mostly because of me. That won't take too much effort to clean up. Just a shower and some clean clothes and we'll be set for the day.

"C-Christmas T-Tree shopping?" I ask in my usual efficient way of getting straight to the point because it takes too long otherwise.

Zak's beautiful face breaks out into a broad grin and he nods. "You bet." He glances down, and Zen, who has waited patiently in his little fur-lined basket while we indulged our animal instincts. "Waddya say, Zen?" the dog's ears twitch at the sound of his name. "Are we gonna get Niall the biggest ass Christmas Tree or what?"

Zen barks, a short sharp reply.

Well, I think I'd better rearrange the furniture in the living room and hope that's all it will take to fit the tree in.

The End

About the Author

Dawn is from the North East of England. Her life is spent juggling. The juggling balls are: children, husband, work (occasionally), voluntary work, professional knitting (notice she doesn't class this as work), and writing. When she has time she actually sleeps.

The whole point of writing for Dawn is just to get it all off her chest and out of her head. If she doesn't write it down then she ends up having long conversations with the characters out loud and her husband thinks she's crazy.

Contact & Media

Twitter: www.twitter.com/dawnsister1

Tumblr: dawnsister.tumblr.com

Facebook: www.facebook.com/DawnSister

Goodreads: www.goodreads.com/DawnSister

Beaten Track: www.beatentrackpublishing.com/dawnsister

By the Author

Dazzled By The Light

The Halloween Incident

See You Smile (Love's Landscapes)

Merry F***cking Christmas

Eagle Man and Mr Hawk (Love is an Open Road)

Not a Word (Love is an Open Road)

Locked in the Moment (Love Unlocked)

A Springful of Winters (Seasons of Love)

By the Author

Beaten Track Publishing

For more titles from Beaten Track Publishing,
please visit our website:

http://www.beatentrackpublishing.com

Thanks for reading!

www.ingramcontent.com/pod-product-compliance
Lightning Source LLC
Chambersburg PA
CBHW022133170626
46808CB00002B/973